WHISKEY SUNRISE

By the Author

All Things Rise

The Ground Beneath

The Time Before Now

Whiskey Sunrise

WHISKEY SUNRISE

by

Missouri Vaun

2016

WHISKEY SUNRISE

ISBN 13: 978-1-62639-519-0

This Trade Paperback Original Is Published By
Bold Strokes Books, Inc.
P.O. Box 249
Valley Falls, NY 12185

First Edition: February 2016

CREDITS
Editor: Cindy Cresap
Production Design: Stacia Seaman
Character Illustration by Paige Braddock
Cover Design by Sheri (graphicartist2020@hotmail.com)

Acknowledgments

This narrative is by far the most personal story I've written. My great-grandfather was a Church of God minister and a moonshiner and saw no conflict between those two pursuits. When I walk the Appalachian Trail in north Georgia today, I can still find the stands of uniform poplars that grew over small gaps between the ridges where he used to raise corn for his still.

Special thanks go out to those who read early drafts of this book and helped me sharpen certain aspects of the story. Jenny, D. Jackson Leigh, Alena, and Vanessa, the writing process would be so much harder without your insights, feedback, and encouragement. Thank you to my beautiful and supportive wife, Evelyn, who is an ever-patient sounding board for scenes that I can't quite figure out.

I'm continually grateful for the team at Bold Strokes Books. Radclyffe, Sandy, Ruth, Cindy, Sheri, the more I work with all of you, the more I like you and the more I appreciate the unique skills each of you brings to the publishing process. The community of writers you've fostered are now folks I consider good friends.

Many details in this book came from true events related to me by my father and grandfather. The demise of certain rural schoolteachers for saying the earth is round being one of them.

And lastly, I'd like to say thank you to my parents. They were able to move past their Southern Baptist upbringing to accept me fully for the person that I am. It took fifteen years after my initial "coming out," but love triumphed, and for that I will be eternally grateful.

For Evelyn

CHAPTER ONE

L ovey pushed through the screen door onto the somewhat uneven boards of the long front porch. The air, warm and damp, carried the scent of honeysuckle. A chorus of jubilant cicadas cut across the shadows from the dense greenery that surrounded her father's house. She stepped off the porch, and sharp tips of grass sorely in need of a trim tickled her ankles and the tops of her feet just below the buckled strap of her shoes as she crossed the lush lawn.

The radio had entertained her for a while, its glowing dial flickering like a lit candle in the darkening room, but even Glenn Miller's orchestra couldn't hold Lovey's attention. Her legs began to ache for movement, like some itch she couldn't quite scratch. She'd checked the kitchen clock before leaving the house. Ten thirty. Late by some standards, but Lovey decided to take a walk anyway.

Any autos that traveled the dirt road in front of her father's place were long gone by this hour. All was quiet except for the tree frogs and cicadas. The complete darkness might have scared some women, but not Lovey. She felt consoled by the darkness, feeling some kinship for the black expanse overhead, as it seemed to echo the darkness she'd been laboring under for the past few months. Darkness felt familiar.

Her father, Reverend Abraham Edwards, was attending some clandestine Baptist deacon's meeting the next county over, and she wasn't sure when he'd return. She'd been alone in the house since early afternoon, moving restlessly from room to room before finally settling in the reading room, near the large oak-encased radio.

Having only just found herself in a situation where she was forced to once again live in her father's strictly run household, Lovey chafed to have her freedom back. Not only that, she missed the life she'd found and lost. She missed George terribly. Was it just a year ago that she'd lost him? The autumn that followed the summer of 1938 was a blur of burial arrangements, grieving, adjustments, and transition. And now 1939 had arrived and was half spent before she'd hardly noticed.

Not only did she mourn for George, she longed for Chicago and the friends she'd made while they were there. They'd huddle for hours debating politics, arguing about communism, socialism, and even democracy. Once they tired of politics, the conversations would turn to poetry and literature. Those moments of elevated discourse were now a faint memory as her life had come crashing down around her and she'd been forced to return to the rural South where the most riveting bit of news seemed to be a shared recipe for peach cobbler or a particularly intricate quilt pattern. With war rampant in Europe, the men in the community seemed to vibrate with the expectation of it. The herald of its coming moved through the air like static electricity, but Southern women, if they had such concerns, seemed to keep silent on the subject.

Her father had arranged an appointment as a teacher in a rural, one-room schoolhouse. She would assume her post in early September. Until then, the summer stretched in front of Lovey like an endless loop that promised only heat, humidity, and her father's long-winded Sunday sermons, followed by covered dish suppers on the church lawn.

Lovey reached the shoulder of the rural throughway and turned left. The gravel crunching underfoot on the dusty road reverberated in her ears like a percussion section for the chorus of night creatures. Every now and then she kicked a stone off the roadway into the tall grass just to see the grasshoppers take flight.

She'd escaped after college, through marriage, to the city, but fate had struck down her dreams and delivered her back home. Only this wasn't a home she'd ever known before. Her father had been called to pastor this rural congregation only six months prior to her return home. She'd forgotten what it was like to live under the glass bubble as a minister's daughter. Lovey was practiced at saying the right thing, doing the right thing, and knowing when to be seen and not heard, but that didn't mean she liked it. Out of respect for her father she'd agreed to play the role of dutiful daughter to the best of her abilities. What choice did she have as long as she was under his roof?

Lovey stopped for a moment to look up at the specks of light piercing the blackness like pinholes from some brighter place just beyond. A shooting star caught her eye as it burned away in the atmosphere. Did she dare make a wish? Wishing would require more faith than she felt she could muster at the moment, but maybe she could conjure a glimmer of hope. Possibilities seemed limited, but she could at least hope.

She hugged herself tightly and continued her stroll.

❖

The wind from the open window whipped through Royal's hair. Driving fast with the windows down was one of her favorite summer pastimes. The radio piped "Moonlight Serenade" through the dark interior of the Ford sedan as she pulled the stick down into third. Adrenaline surged through her body as the flathead V-8 hit its stride along the straightaway of the freshly graded county road. The occasional pop of a rock thrown by the tires banged against the steel undercarriage disrespectfully intruding on Glenn Miller's smooth melody.

At this late hour, Royal Duval was usually trippin' a load of moonshine, but not tonight. She'd promised her cousin Ned she'd run the car on a different course. Just to test a new shortcut and the car, before making the run with a full load. Ned wanted a ride-along, but Royal preferred to test drive alone. So far, she liked the modifications he'd made on her stock '39 Ford. She'd use the word *screamer* if she didn't think it'd go straight to his head. The engine had been bored, fitted with three carburetors, and extra helper springs in the suspension for runs when she'd be carrying heavy liquid cargo to Hall County or farther south to Atlanta.

It was a little past eleven o'clock, and Royal hadn't seen another car on the road since she left Highway Nine heading back through Dawsonville toward the hills. The night was clear but very dark. The circles of light provided her only visibility preceding the Ford's breakneck speed down the winding dirt road. Royal downshifted and braked as she rounded a bend, throwing rocks as the two-door sedan crossed the center point in the road. Just as the headlights crested the blind curve, an apparition appeared at the shoulder.

Damn! She jerked the wheel in an attempt to miss the ghostly figure flash lit by the headlights.

As the heavy Ford slid through the turn, there was just enough of a rut at the road's edge to snag the front wheel, hindering Royal's ability to right the car's trajectory. Time seemed suspended as the auto skidded, bounced over the shoulder, lost its center of gravity, and rolled down the slight grade on the outside of the curve.

The throaty combustion of eight pounding cylinders roared as the sedan's tires left the ground in an airborne spiral. Inside the car, Royal gripped the wheel with one hand and braced her other hand against the high, curved roof, for a moment suspended, weightless.

CHAPTER TWO

L ovey saw the glow of headlights just seconds before the sedan bore down on her. She heard a roar followed by a blinding light. She stood frozen for an instant, rooted like a light-struck deer, unable to move as the speeding sedan swerved to miss her. She lunged off the road toward the steep embankment on the inside of the curve just as the car veered away from her and tumbled down the slight grade away from the road.

Lovey was lying against the damp earth. Her heart beat wildly. It took another moment for her to gather her shocked senses before she ran to the crest of the hill to look for the car. From her vantage point, she could hear the engine sputter and stall. And she could see the large dark sedan, in its upended position, wheels spinning freely in a cloud of dust, the headlights pointed skyward, illuminating nothing but tree branches.

Deftly and as fast as she could move over the now rutted uneven turf, Lovey ran down to check the driver.

When she came along the side of the car she could make out the shadowed silhouette of a struggling figure, hanging upside down from the driver's seat.

"Are you all right? Are you hurt?" Lovey asked. She was slightly breathless from her quick descent and the fright of almost being run over. Death by auto was certainly not the wish she'd made, nor the possibility she'd been hoping for.

"I'm okay, but my foot is caught."

It was dark in the car's interior so Lovey couldn't make out details, but despite masculine clothing, the voice that spoke sounded young, maybe even feminine. Lovey puzzled over this as she jerked at the door handle a few times before getting it to release. Once the door was open, she leaned inside.

"Let me help you." It was so dark that Lovey was having a hard time figuring out exactly how the driver was stuck.

"My boot lace is wrapped around the brake, I think. I've got a folding knife in my pocket. If you could get it then you could cut me loose." The driver was struggling to keep still, balanced between the seat and the roof of the car. "If I let go I might break my ankle from the weight, or worse, my neck."

"I'm not reaching into some strange boy's trousers."

"There's no boy here unless you brought one with you." The stranger smiled, despite the circumstances, seemingly amused by the mistaken identity.

"Oh, I'm sorry. I just assumed based on the way you're dressed—"

"How about we debate the finer points of fashion once you cut me loose?"

Lovey was reluctant to undertake such an intimate task as rummaging in the front pocket of some stranger's trousers, but she didn't see any way around it. She thrust her fingers into the driver's pocket and felt around for the knife.

"Careful. I'm gettin' a little excited."

"What?" Lovey recoiled, exasperated. "Look, do you want me to leave you hanging there or do you want my help?"

"I'm sorry, truly. It's just all the blood is running to my head. It's making me punchy. Please cut me loose."

Lovey reluctantly resumed her search. She found the knife, then practically had to climb inside the car in order to reach the foot pedals to cut the tangled bootlace.

The instant the tension on the cord was released, the full weight of the driver collapsed against Lovey, and the two of them tumbled out of the car in a heap. Lovey found herself suddenly in contact with the trouser-clad young woman, the hem of her dress askew and the woman's head in her lap. She peered up at Lovey, a dazed look in her eyes. Lovey felt the woman shiver against her, despite the warm summer night. Obviously, in spite of her bravado, the wreck had shaken her up. They didn't touch, other than where her head rested in Lovey's lap, but the direct gaze that passed between them sent a pulsing sensation through Lovey's chest that caused her to catch her breath.

The driver scooted back toward the side of the upturned vehicle.

"Thank you." The woman pushed a thick tuft of blond hair back from her forehead. Her hands were trembling even though she appeared to be trying to conceal that fact by rubbing them up and down her thighs.

"You're welcome. And I think you're bleeding." Lovey watched as the woman touched her brow where blood was seeping from a cut. The car's headlights were still pointed up into the trees, which offered a small amount of reflected light on the ground below.

Lovey rose quickly, dusting off her dress, as the stranger stood, swayed, and leaned back against the open car door. "Maybe you hit the steering wheel," Lovey said.

"Must have."

"Are you hurt anywhere else?"

"I don't think so." She gave Lovey a slightly pained look. "But I think I'm a little shaky on my feet."

"Do you feel well enough to walk? I live very close. Why don't we walk back to my house and see about that cut over your eye? Then we can call someone about your car." Lovey offered the invitation without really thinking through the possible consequences of inviting a complete stranger back to her house. It dawned on her that her father would likely not be home for another hour, maybe two. But it was too late to recant the invitation now.

"Thank you again. I'm Royal Duval, by the way." Royal extended a hand and then realized her palm was covered with blood, which she wiped on her khaki trousers. "Sorry. I think I got blood on your dress."

Lovey looked down for the first time at the stain on her dress where Royal's head had landed. Those smudges along with smears of red clay where she'd hugged the dirt embankment comingled in such a way that a bystander might have surmised she'd been in the crash along with Royal instead of watching it from the roadway.

She sighed and wiped ineffectively at the dirt smudges. "I'm Lovey Porter, and my father's place is just back up the road a few minutes. Come on." Royal nodded, briefly turning to switch off the headlights and retrieve the car key before shutting the door and allowing Lovey to steer her up the hill by the elbow.

Lovey marveled at the turn her evening had taken as they trudged slowly back to the roadway. Royal stumbled, which called Lovey back to the present moment. She put an arm around her waist. "Should we stop for a minute?"

"No, I'm fine. Just a little shaken up. It'll pass." Royal took in a deep breath and let it out. "I'll be okay."

Lovey removed her arm but kept it near Royal's back in case she faltered again.

CHAPTER THREE

After a few initially wobbly steps, Lovey was pleased that the walk back to the house was uneventful. Royal was probably more frightened than she was willing to admit to a total stranger. Lovey would have been surprised if she hadn't been, given the tumble she'd just taken. The light on the porch was still lit as Lovey pulled the screen door open and motioned for Royal to enter.

"Wait here for a minute while I turn on a light inside." Lovey moved past Royal and flipped a switch in the kitchen. The light from the adjoining room cast a soft glow over the foyer where Royal was still standing. Lovey ushered her into the kitchen.

Royal was leaning against the sink, looking around as Lovey moved closer. Standing in front of her, Lovey found herself captivated by the bluest eyes she'd ever seen. Royal's sun-kissed skin and blond, short-cropped hair, in spots, almost bleached white, no doubt from hours in the sun, set off her eyes perfectly. Royal seemed to realize Lovey was studying her and self-consciously attempted to tuck in her unruly shirttail. The white collared shirt had marks and a few spots of blood on it now. It was loosely tucked back into tan men's trousers, held up by suspenders. Royal's build was slim, but not slight. Lovey thought the men's clothes suited her slender frame well.

Somehow, knowing the stranger she'd rescued from the car was a woman, Lovey felt braver about the decision to bring her back to the house. Royal was like no one she'd ever met before. Lovey had to admit she was intrigued.

Emboldened, Lovey stepped closer still and reached to brush the hair away from Royal's forehead to get a better look at the cut. Lovey noticed Royal flinch. She paused before actually making contact. "Is it okay if I take a look?"

They were almost the same height. Royal might have been an inch or two taller, and standing close the way they were at the moment, their eyes locked and Lovey's heart fluttered unexpectedly. *There it is again. What is that about?*

Royal nodded in reply, and Lovey gently brushed the errant bit of hair away from the wound.

❖

Royal's skin tingled from the brush of Lovey's fingers. They were standing so close that when Royal released a soft sigh, Lovey's bobbed, wavy hair stirred around her soft features. She'd been studying Royal with dark eyes, and the only word Royal could call forth to describe the sensation was *exposed*. After examining the still bleeding cut just above her eyebrow, Lovey scrunched her nose and took a step back. Lovey pushed her thick hair back from her face. Her hair was shorter than the way most of the local girls wore theirs, cropped just at her jawline, thick and full of waves. Lovey had the biggest, softest brown eyes Royal had ever seen. The sort of bottomless pools a person could get lost in. Her lips seemed to be perpetually turned up just at the corners as if she'd just heard a good joke and couldn't wait to share it.

Her figure was slim with slight girlish curves. The dress she wore hung loosely, the waistline dropping below her hips just the way they wore them in magazines. Obviously, Lovey had landed here from some other place than the hills and hollows of Dawson County. For surely had she existed here previously, Royal most certainly would have noticed.

"Wait here. I'll get something to clean that up and I'll be right back. Why don't you sit down?" Lovey motioned toward a kitchen chair as she left the room.

With Lovey no longer in her personal space, Royal slumped

against the sink for a minute and exhaled. Moving slowly, she took a seat. Heels clicking on the hardwood floor signaled Lovey's return to the kitchen. She was carrying a small box of gauze, tape, an iodine bottle, and a cloth.

Royal watched as Lovey placed the items on the table and turned toward the sink to dampen the cloth before pulling up a chair. Her movements were fluid. Royal couldn't help but notice the pale skin of her slender arms exposed beneath the short sleeves of the blue cotton dress, and her long, tapered fingers. Lovey cupped Royal's chin in one hand as she gently dabbed at the cut with the damp cloth in her other hand. She was so close that Royal could smell lavender on her skin. There she was again, in Royal's space, making Royal's ears and cheeks heat up and her heart rate increase. She was used to being the confident one in almost any situation, but clearly, Lovey was just as confident. This made Royal more than a little nervous.

Seeming satisfied that the cut was clean, Lovey reached for the iodine bottle.

"This will probably sting just a bit." Royal nodded, and Lovey began to dab the red-brown liquid over the cut. It did sting, and Lovey tenderly blew on it after each dab. Even her breath smelled sweet, and Royal worried she was in danger of passing out, not from the injury but from the proximity of this particular caregiver.

Lovey rocked back in her chair. She'd just put a small piece of gauze over the wound and taped it in place. "How do you feel?"

"Fine." Royal's throat was dry and her voice cracked. "Good."

"Water?" offered Lovey.

"Yes, please."

"Or I may even have lemonade."

"Even better." Royal cleared her throat as Lovey pulled glasses from the cabinet and filled them from a pitcher near the sink. After quenching her thirst and attempting to calm her nerves, Royal shifted in her chair and looked around the house a little. She could see a glimpse of the living room from where she sat and noted that it was comfortably full of upholstered furniture, small tables, and books, lots of books.

"Do you like to read?" Royal sipped as she turned back to Lovey.

"Most of those belong to my father. He's a minister and he uses lots of references for his sermons." It dawned on Royal where she was. Maybe she'd taken a harder lick to the head than she'd realized, or maybe she'd just been too distracted by Lovey's attentions to think clearly.

"Your father is Reverend Edwards?"

"You know him?" Lovey regarded Royal as she sipped lemonade.

"I know of him." But the last names didn't match. That's why Royal hadn't put the facts together. "Didn't you say your last name was Porter?"

"Porter is my married name."

"Oh." Hope sank in Royal's chest like a rock dropped into a shallow pond. Even though she'd known it was foolish to consider it, she'd hoped to get a chance to know Lovey better. That wouldn't happen exactly as she'd envisioned if Lovey had a husband in tow.

"My husband died a year ago. I just moved here."

Royal was immediately sorry for thinking ill of a man she didn't even know and now she'd just heard was deceased. "My condolences for your loss."

An awkward silence hung between them in the warmly lit kitchen. The choruses of tree frogs drifted in through the open kitchen window, and a sheer, lace trimmed curtain drifted in the breeze. After another moment, Royal stood up abruptly, the chair skidding back noisily on the wood floor.

"I should go." She'd stood up too quickly though and regretted it as her head began to spin. Lovey was on her feet swiftly, placing a hand on each of Royal's arms to steady her.

❖

Lovey eased Royal back down into the chair. She wasn't quite ready for this encounter to be over, and even if she had been, Royal didn't seem stable enough to strike out without some assistance.

"Why don't we call someone to come get you? My father has a telephone."

"That'd be a great idea, but there'd be no phone to ring on the other end."

"Oh." Lovey considered other options for a moment. "I'd offer to drive you, but Father has the car and I don't know when he'll be back."

"I can walk. It's only a couple of miles to town." Royal attempted to stand again, but quickly sat back down. "Sorry. My head is swimming a little."

"Won't someone notice if you're not home and come looking for you?" Lovey knew that if she'd failed to return home when expected her father would have the entire congregation scouring the tri-county region until they found her.

"No, they'll just assume I stayed in town. I have a rented room there, and if I'm out late, um, working, then sometimes I stay there."

Lovey wondered briefly what work would keep Royal out this late, but she filed that question away for later.

"You were just in a bad accident. I don't think you're in any shape to walk." Lovey didn't really want to let Royal out of her sight. Not while she seemed this shaken up from the wreck. She placed her hand over Royal's resting on the table and caressed it unconsciously. Only when she saw Royal looking down to where her hand covered Royal's did she pull hers away. But in that instant of contact she'd made her decision. "I think you should stay here tonight and I'll drive you home tomorrow."

"What?" Royal regarded Lovey with surprise. "I don't think—"

"I won't let you leave in this condition by yourself, and there's no other way to get you home at the moment. We have a spare room and it's yours for the night." Lovey watched a series of emotions play out across Royal's striking features and wished at that moment she had the ability to read minds. "It's already quite late. I really do think this is the most prudent solution."

"Are you sure the reverend, I mean, your father, won't mind?"

"Well, he's not here to ask, is he? And there's nothing of higher value than Christian charity for those in need, is there?" Although, even while trying to convince herself charity was at the root of the invitation, Lovey knew that wasn't the entire truth. She felt something for Royal that she couldn't yet name. The air seemed to vibrate between them, and she hadn't felt this alive in months. She'd been sequestering herself in the house for weeks after making the trip from Chicago. Tonight was the first night in forever that gave her any feeling that there might be a life out there in the world she'd want to experience. Lovey had no idea how or why meeting Royal had flipped some switch on inside her mournful existence, but she wanted to find out.

Lovey extended her hand to Royal. "I think you should lie down. It's a short walk to the spare room." Once they arrived, Royal sat on the side of the bed and Lovey offered to help remove her shoes. She worried that if Royal attempted to bend over to loosen what remained of the laces in her boots she might topple headfirst to the floor.

After Royal's shoes were off and stowed near the door, Lovey sat beside Royal on the bed. They were turned so that they partially faced each other, and Lovey began to unbutton Royal's soiled shirt as if it were the most normal thing in the world to do. Royal didn't seem to mind the attention, and after all, they were both women, so what did it matter if she saw Royal in a state of undress down to her undershirt and trousers? After unbuttoning the shirt, she slid her hands under the suspenders and slipped them from Royal's thin, broad shoulders. The gesture felt intimate in a way she hadn't intended. Lovey's heart began to pound in her chest, and she looked up to see Royal regard her curiously.

"Why were you walking alone on the road this late at night?" Royal's voice was soft and the question seemed to hold no judgment, only genuine curiosity.

Lovey was quiet for a moment as she fingered the placket of Royal's open shirt. "Do you ever feel like spaces are closing in on you?"

Royal was silent, so Lovey continued. It had been so long since someone had asked her anything truly personal. She was sick and tired of condolences and folks tiptoeing around her sadness. Death scared people. And there was nothing anyone could say that helped ease the hurt anyway.

"I needed to be out in the night." Lovey allowed her gaze to focus on a loose button at the front of Royal's shirt. "Somehow, the darkness comforts me, maybe because I can't see the edge of it. And the infinite curve of the stars, while it does make me feel small, it also makes me feel like I'm part of something so much larger. Something so large that it's untouched by my earthly concerns."

Lovey watched Royal slip her arms free of her smudged shirt, her tanned shoulders extended past the tank cut T-shirt that remained.

"I'm sorry. You've just been in an accident and I'm rambling." Lovey took the shirt from Royal and stood to hang it over a nearby chair. They had not lit the lamp in the bedroom, but indirect light spilled through the open door from the kitchen just down the hall.

"You're not rambling. I asked."

"You should rest." Lovey lifted a folded quilt from the foot of the bed as Royal lay back on the pillow. Lovey pulled the handmade covering up over her still trouser clad legs to her waist. "Do you need anything else?"

"No, you've been extremely kind given I nearly ran you over."

"But you didn't. You sacrificed yourself instead." Lovey tucked the covers around Royal. "And for that I'm very grateful."

She lingered in the open door before pulling it softly closed behind her. "Good night, Royal."

"Good night, Lovey."

CHAPTER FOUR

Royal thought there'd be no way she'd fall asleep knowing Lovey was just down the hall, but she did. The pink hue of the approaching sunrise was just peeking through the window of the spare room when Royal roused. For a moment, she couldn't remember where she was. She was lying under a quilt pattern she didn't recognize, still partially dressed. She sat up and then her pounding head sent her a quick reminder. The wreck. She'd left her car upside down at the base of a large tree, and she'd spent the night in Reverend Abraham Edwards's house. The only person in the tri-county area who professed to abhor moonshine more than the local revenuers was Reverend Edwards, and she was about to meet him at the breakfast table if she didn't pull herself together and make a quick escape.

Royal paused for a moment as she was pulling on her boots, having to stabilize herself against the footboard. She took a long, slow breath, retrieved her shirt from a nearby chair, and pulled it on. Looking back at the bed, she decided to fold the quilt before climbing out the window. Lovey would no doubt wonder why she'd snuck off so early, but Royal felt confident she'd be glad at the same time. The last guest Lovey needed at the kitchen table was a known moonshine runner. She tried to be as silent as possible in the dim early morning light as she slid the window open and dropped between some rather stiff shrubberies.

She cursed in hushed whispers as she pulled stiff twigs from under her shirttail and extricated herself from the bushes. A light came on in a window several feet away from where she stood, which inspired Royal to make quick steps away from the house toward the road.

The two-mile walk into town did little to quiet her mind. Over and over, she ran the details through her head trying to figure out if Lovey had been flirting with her or just being nice, or maybe a little of both. If luck was on her side she'd find Frank before deliveries and catch a ride to her house, then later Ned could help her retrieve the car.

Frank was toting a large sack of feed out to a buckboard just as she walked up. Luck was on her side after all.

"Good Lord, Royal. Looks like you had a rough night." Frank leaned on the feed sack he'd just deposited in the back of the horse-drawn wagon.

Her shirt was soiled, there was a bandage over her eye, and one boot clomped as she walked due to its shortened lace. "Actually, it coulda been worse."

"Well, this is a story I've gotta hear."

"Can you give me a lift home?" Royal was beat and didn't feel like walking another mile to her mother's place.

"Sure, take a seat. I've got one more thing to load and then we can be on our way."

Royal nodded and gratefully climbed up onto the wooden bench seat at the front of the wagon and waited for Frank to return.

❖

Lovey woke with a start, remembering that she'd invited Royal to stay over in the spare room. She pulled on a robe and padded down the hallway in her bare feet. She peeked into the guest room. Empty. She took note of the folded quilt at the foot of the bed.

"Would you like some coffee?" her father called to her from the kitchen.

Her heart rate increased for a moment at the thought of Royal and her father having coffee together. She was oddly relieved when she entered the kitchen and saw him seated by himself reading his Bible.

"I'll get it, thank you." Lovey poured herself a cup and stood leaning against the counter. "You're studying already?"

"Couldn't sleep."

"Really?"

"I thought I heard someone outside the house, in the bushes this morning. Once I woke up I couldn't get back to sleep so I figured I might as well get started on this week's sermon."

Surely Royal didn't climb out the window? But maybe she had. The image of Royal sneaking out the window like an illicit lover and almost getting caught by her father amused her.

"What are you smiling about?" Lovey's father regarded her with a curious expression.

"Oh, nothing. Why don't I make us some breakfast?"

"You're hungry?" Her father closed the black leather cover of the enormous Bible in front of him and slouched back in his chair. He removed the wire-rimmed spectacles from his prominent nose, giving her his full attention. She thought her father had aged quite a bit since she'd been away in Chicago. He was always a slender, bookish man, but somehow he seemed thinner, maybe even stooped a little at the shoulders. His thinning gray hair was a bit unkempt first thing in the morning.

"Yes, I suppose I am hungry."

"You seem different this morning. Did something happen last night?"

Lovey realized that he was right. She felt different. She almost felt happy, and for the first time in months, she actually had an appetite. She wanted to eat rather than having to force herself to eat something.

"No, nothing special happened. I just went for a walk and it was a lovely night. How many eggs would you like?" Lovey turned to look at her father before she opened the icebox.

❖

Royal waved back at Frank as she headed up the steps. Her mother was in the kitchen pulling biscuits out of the cast iron stove as she pushed through the door. The smell of hot buttermilk biscuits hung in the air. She figured if heaven had a scent this would be it. Her stomach growled in response.

"Royal, is that you?" her mother asked.

"Yeah." She settled into a chair at the table, a bit exhausted by her escape and walk into town. Her head ached, her heel was surely blistered from her boot slipping with every step, and she now realized she was starving. What an impressive mess. *No wonder Lovey thought I needed assistance.*

The large black iron pan clanged loudly on the stovetop, causing Royal to jump like a spooked rabbit. Her mother regarded her with a look that seemed to be a mixture of fear and anger. She knew what was coming next and chided herself for not cleaning up before coming into the house.

"Lillian Royal Duval, what in God's name have you gotten into? Have you been in a fight? Did you wreck your car?" Her mother's voice got progressively louder with each question.

"I bumped my head is all." Royal's mind raced ahead of her words as she attempted to conjure up a believable story that would bear no resemblance to what had actually happened. "Ned and I were goofing around in town at the tavern and I fell. You know what a dead hoofer I am."

"I've never seen you dance poorly enough to knock yourself silly. Don't lie to me, Royal."

"Momma, I'm tellin' the truth. I got distracted by this girl, and the next thing I knew my feet were all tripped up and I banged my head on a table as I went down." The sincerity she could muster for a complete fabrication amazed her. Maybe because her encounter with Lovey had made her dizzy, but she reckoned the rest of the story was more to protect her mother from the truth than to be dishonest. This occasion had to be the one instance when telling a lie was the more honorable thing to do.

When she was a child, her father had been killed in a similar accident. The last thing she wanted was to frighten her mother by telling her she'd rolled the Ford. Her cousin Ned would help her get the car back on four wheels and no one would be the wiser.

"You chasing girls is gonna be the death of me." Her mother huffed, bracing her fists against her hips.

While her mother would likely never completely embrace Royal's boyish dress or her attraction to women, at least she'd come to terms with it on some level. Royal had been incredibly stubborn as a child, or so she'd been told. Her mother had stopped trying to coerce Royal into wearing dresses by age nine.

Her mother had been equally tolerant of the long spells Royal spent hidden away in her room. *What have you been doing in there for so long*, her mother would ask upon her emergence. *Thinking and writing things down,* would be Royal's response.

She'd discovered a book, a collection of selected poems, in her father's things one afternoon, and ever since had been captivated by poetry. Royal would pronounce to her family that poetry didn't tell you how to think, it told you how to feel. Royal was lucky that both her mother and her grandfather let her find her own path.

"Go wake your brother. He's got chores to do." Her mother spoke over her shoulder as she stirred eggs in a pan.

Royal begrudgingly got to her feet. After all, she'd just sat down and still hadn't managed to snag one of those hot biscuits. "And put on a clean shirt before you come back to the table," her mother shouted.

Royal stepped into her brother's room and shoved the bed frame with her boot. "Teddy, get up. Breakfast is ready."

Her brother moaned but didn't move.

"Get up!"

"Stop shakin' the bed, Royal. I'm up." She couldn't see his face, hidden in the covers, but she heard his muffled voice.

"Don't make me toss you out of that bed."

He pulled the covers back so she could see his annoyed look. "Don't make me toss you outta this room."

"Okay, okay. I'll tell Momma you're coming soon." Theodore Duval was sixteen going on twelve in Royal's opinion. In their father's absence, their mother babied him no end, so she felt like it was her sisterly duty to toughen him up. Or at least try. She'd experienced only limited success in this endeavor, as he was very sensitive for a boy. He'd cry at the drop of a hat when he was a kid, and in his daily life was far more empathetic to others than anyone she knew. She hoped he'd choose a different path away from the family business because she feared he was too kindhearted for the moonshine trade. She did her best to shield him from it, but that didn't mean she wouldn't give him a sisterly hard time now and again.

As he lingered under the covers, she silently slipped the lace out of one of his boots before heading upstairs to her room for fresh clothes.

A few minutes later, Royal returned to the warmth of the kitchen, finishing the last button on her clean shirt as she sat down. Teddy sleepily dropped into the chair across from her and reached for a biscuit. Their mother slapped his hand. With his tousled, short blond hair and tanned, sharp features, he looked like a slightly younger, slightly lankier version of Royal.

"As long as I'm in this house we'll say grace before we eat." Their mother clasped her hands together and gave them both a withering look.

"Yes, ma'am." Teddy settled back, folded his hands, and closed his eyes.

CHAPTER FIVE

Lovey had just finished washing the breakfast dishes when Cal came through the front door. Cal was a local woman that her father had taken on for cleaning, cooking, and washing. Since Lovey had returned she'd taken to cooking certain meals but was thankful to have Cal's help for all the other tasks around the house. When she'd first arrived, Lovey had been so depressed that she'd hardly left her room. She figured she owed Cal's fine cooking for keeping her alive during that sad transition.

Cal had smooth, dark skin, and her full figure was a testament to her skill in the kitchen. Her cakes were legend. More than one young bride in the county in need of a wedding cake had hired her.

"Good morning, Cal." Lovey hung the drying towel near the sink.

"Morning, Miss Lovey." Cal set her purse and a brown paper sack of groceries on the table. Her dark eyes followed Lovey as she moved to leave the kitchen. "Are you goin' out, Miss Lovey?"

"Um, yes, I thought I'd take a walk." Lovey noticed the surprised expression on Cal's face. Had she really been that much of a recluse the past few weeks? Maybe. Lovey leaned against the door frame as Cal unpacked the groceries and stowed them in the pantry.

"Is Cal your real name?" Lovey felt remiss that she'd been spending time with Cal for months and had never asked this question before.

"It's Callalily, but everyone has always called me Cal."

"That's a beautiful name. And a beautiful flower."

Cal stopped what she was doing and gave Lovey her full attention. "You seem different today, Miss Lovey."

"Do I?"

"Yes, miss, and I'm glad to see it. You seem lighter. Whatever it is you've been up to, you should keep doin' it."

Lovey smiled. "I'll definitely take that under advisement, Cal." First her father and now Cal had mentioned a shift in her demeanor. *I do feel lighter.*

"I'll see you later. If my father asks, will you just tell him I'll be back shortly?" She turned and left Cal to her tasks.

She puzzled over her own shift in mood as she stepped off the porch and began her walk. She turned left when she reached the road, headed back to where she'd seen Royal's car go over the bank. She hoped the car would still be there, which meant she might see Royal again. As she neared the turn, she saw there was an old pickup truck with wooden slats in the sides parked on the shoulder.

As she reached the crest of the curve, near the parked truck, Lovey registered her heart rate increase. The upturned car looked scarier in the full light of day. Royal was standing down near the upended sedan, her white shirt contrasted against the dark auto, her posture pensive.

With the boyish clothes, Lovey would have definitely described Royal as a tomboy, but would never have described her as masculine. There was something decidedly feminine about Royal that she'd noticed the previous night in the kitchen. Her features, while strong, were unmistakably feminine. Royal had high cheekbones and heart-stopping blue eyes, shadowed by long lashes. Lovey had taken in all these details the night before and was now enjoying the view from a small distance. Despite feminine features, Royal's stance was confident and assured; it carried an element of self-confidence usually only observed in young men.

Motion caught Lovey's eye. Royal wasn't alone. Two young men were nearby attaching a system of pulleys and a winch to the upturned car. Lovey decided to step behind some trees and watch.

As she observed the men work, Royal held her thumb at her

mouth as if she'd just been in some deep thought. Noticing this detail only served to pull Lovey's attention to Royal's lips, her mouth. Allowing her gaze to linger there for a moment caused her insides to stir in an unexpected way. Aware that she was staring but as yet unseen by Royal, Lovey decided to step a little closer behind a different tree so that she could better see the goings-on undetected.

Finding Royal's face more than a little distracting, she refocused her attention on Royal as a whole. The fresh white shirt and pressed, clean trousers made Lovey wonder who waited at home for Royal. That the question had entered her mind at all struck her as unusual. Who was it that cared for Royal and waited up for her at night? Or was she alone in the world? Royal had said that if she didn't return home from time to time that no one would worry. Remembering that statement made Lovey feel sad.

Lovey stood, sheltered from view just below the crest of the small rise watching Royal and the two young men working below to reorient the Ford sedan. Had the car tumbled a few more times it could easily have ended up in the pond that lay just beyond where the car had come to rest on its roof. An underwater rescue might have been much more dangerous in the dark. Maybe even life threatening. Lovey shuddered at the thought of it.

Royal cranked the pulley and increased the pressure on the cables. She was wearing only an undershirt now, her collared shirt thrown over a nearby shrub, no doubt in an attempt to keep it clean. Royal's tanned arms had a slight glow from the exertion of cranking increased tension on the pulley. The two men were on the other side of the car pushing in the same direction that the cables were tugging. The sound of rocks scraping metal followed the motion of the large sedan as it rocked slowly back to its rightful orientation. The car thumped heavily onto all four wheels in a cloud of dust. The cables, now slack, dropped into the dirt in front of Royal. Had the car not come to rest at an angle, almost on its side, the tow cable might not have had enough torque to pull the auto over.

One of the young men clearly had a family resemblance to Royal. The second young man, dark-skinned, tall, skinny, and clad in overalls that had been worn so thin they'd lost most of their color, circled around the car to check the damage. He began to gather up the equipment and stowed it in the back of an old Model A truck parked near the dark sedan.

Lovey could no longer see Royal from her hiding spot behind the wild hydrangea. She felt silly, hiding like a teenager. *For goodness sake, I'm a twenty-six-year-old woman, hiding like a schoolgirl.*

She shifted to her left a little and leaned around the base of a large spruce about to make her presence known. But before she could announce herself by saying hello, she felt a fuzzy tickling inside her skirt. And then a second. And then a third.

And then the first sting! Yellow jackets! She'd stood on a nest in the ground and they were buzzing around inside the draped light cotton fabric of her dress. *Oh, no! No! No! No!* She practically jumped out of her skin from the second sting.

Lovey yelped and danced around, stomping her feet to dislodge the aggressive insects. Then she took off running, all the while swatting at her lower half, but it was doing no good. The bees were in a frenzy now, traveling with her, under her skirt and stinging whenever they found a piece of skin to light on. A flurry of arms and elbows, she sped off down the hill toward the pond. Not caring who was nearby, Lovey raised her skirt up, exposing her skivvies and legs to anyone who was within earshot of her squeals.

She screamed as she tore past them waving her arms madly. In a full-on frightful fit, she sprinted toward the pond with her skirt practically pulled up over her head, shoes flying off as she took the last bounding leap, like a wild woman, into the pond.

❖

Royal jerked her head up from under the hood of the Ford just in time to see Lovey with flailing arms tear past where they stood. She hadn't even seen Lovey walk up and had no idea where she'd come from. The two young men standing near her followed Lovey's trajectory with surprised amusement.

"Who in tarnation was that?" Ned wiped grease from his hands on a rag he kept in his back pocket.

"That was the girl who rescued me last night, Lovey Porter." Royal leaned around Ned just in time to catch a glimpse of her light blue skirt as she made a running leap into the pond.

"Well, she seems a bit touched in the head, but she's got nice legs," said Ned.

Royal punched Ned in the shoulder. "I think I'd best go check on her."

"I should go with you and make sure she doesn't need help."

Ned and Royal left the open hood and trotted to the pond where Lovey was treading water sunk up to her chin. Sam hung back by the car. After a moment, he walked toward the pond, but at a slower pace.

"Did you have the sudden urge for a swim?" Royal crossed her arms in front of her chest as she stood on the bank.

"Say, miss, do you need assistance?" asked Ned.

"Lovey, this is my cousin, Ned, and the other fellow up the hill is Sam. They were just helping me tip the car over. Which you might have noticed as you ran by if your skirt hadn't been over your head." She turned and motioned toward the pond. Sam stood a few feet behind them, seeming to give Lovey a bit more respectful distance. "Ned, Sam, this is Lovey Porter."

"Nice to meet you." Lovey paddled a little closer to the pond's edge but stayed hidden under the water's surface.

"Are you all right?" asked Royal.

"Yellow jackets."

"What?"

"I said I stepped on a yellow jacket nest."

"I'm so sorry." Royal was trying hard not to laugh but failing.

"It's not funny." Lovey splashed around as she treaded water.

"Okay, fellas, why don't you leave me to assist Miss Porter? I don't think she's going to get out of the water with you standing here." Royal motioned with her thumb for them to head back up the hill.

"Why not? I think we pretty much saw the whole show already." Ned pretended to plant his feet as if he wasn't going to leave.

"Go on!" Royal shoved him playfully. "Git!"

"C'mon, then, Ned." Sam tugged at Ned's arm.

Royal called after them. "I'll see you later back at the house."

Ned waved a hand in her direction. Lovey was still submerged, observing the entire exchange from her watery roost. Royal stood watching her until they heard the Ford's V-8 engine roar to life. Royal turned and waved as the vehicle headed up the slight grade and back onto the road.

"Hang on. I'll be right back." Royal trotted back up the hill and pulled the old wood slatted truck closer to the pond and into the shade.

"It's awful hot. Maybe I should join you." Royal hadn't put her collared shirt back on. She began to slip out of her trousers and then she waded into the water in a tank T-shirt and boy's style boxy undershorts. The long-hanging shorts had buttons at the front and drawstrings at the sides. She pushed off the bank and swam out to the center of the pond where Lovey was still treading water.

"I'm so embarrassed." Lovey blew bubbles over the surface.

"You shouldn't be. You did the right thing." Royal skimmed her arms back and forth across the surface a few feet away. "Bees are serious business. They hurt like hell."

They paddled around each other for a moment not talking. Then Royal swam a little closer. "Are the bites still stinging?"

"A little."

"If you let me I could put some wet clay on the bites. It'll pull the stinging out."

"I'm soaked through."

"I've got a blanket I could spread out near the truck in the shade." Still facing Lovey, Royal started swimming backward toward the bank where the truck was parked.

Chapter Six

L ovey knew that if she climbed out of the water, the soaked, thin cotton dress would leave little to the imagination, but she figured there was no way to avoid that now. She followed Royal to shore and stood, arms across her chest, while Royal spread a blanket out for them on a patch of thick grass between the truck and the pond. This spot was far enough away from the crest of the road and additionally sheltered from view by a small grove of live oaks.

"Here, sit down and let me have a look." Royal was kneeling next to an open space on the blanket. Lovey settled herself as best she could, shyly aware of how her wet clothing clung to her torso and breasts. Her hair was mostly dry except at the ends where she pushed it self-consciously away from her flushed cheeks.

Rivulets of water ran across Royal's shoulders and down her arm. She was just as exposed through her thin tank style T-shirt as Lovey, but somehow seemed less bothered by it. Her soaked shorts clung tightly to her thighs as she stood and moved to the red clay at the edge of the pond. She returned after a moment, stirring the dampened red earth around in the palm of her hand.

"Show me where they got you and I'll dab some of this on." Royal knelt next to Lovey.

"Here." Lovey pulled the fabric of her skirt up to reveal a red welt on her calf. "And here." She pulled the dress up further. Two more stings glowed, hotly raised against the pale skin on her thighs.

"Wow, they really got you good." Royal dipped her finger into the pool of soft clay in her palm and tenderly dabbed it over the sites of injury.

Royal was kneeling so close that Lovey could feel the heat off her skin. She knew warmth was spreading through her entire body from their nearness. Why did she have such a strong physical reaction to Royal? Lovey studied Royal's features as she continued to apply the soothing mixture to the bee stings up and down Lovey's legs.

"There. I think I got them all." Royal rocked back on her heels and smiled at Lovey.

"Thank you," whispered Lovey. She found her voice and spoke a little louder, clearing her throat. "Thank you, Royal."

"Would you like something to drink? I brought some things in the truck." Lovey nodded and Royal stood to retrieve a basket from the front seat through the open door of the beat up old truck. "I had planned to stop by your place to see if you wanted to go for a ride. And to apologize for leaving the way I did this morning."

"I was a little surprised by your absence. I was expecting to see you."

"I figured it'd be better if I met your father under more pleasant circumstances. I was sort of a mess this morning."

Lovey reached over and brushed a fallen clump of hair away from the bandage on Royal's forehead.

This time Royal didn't flinch, but rather smiled at Lovey. "I'm having the strangest sensation of déjà vu."

"Are you?"

"It seems like I was in this same spot last night, talking to a girl."

"What sort of girl?"

"Pretty. Mysterious. Kindhearted."

Lovey tried with limited success to ignore Royal's flirtatious tone. "How do you know she was kind?"

"Well, she took me home and bandaged my head." Royal tentatively touched the gauze over her eyebrow. "Oh, and gave me lemonade." At that, Lovey couldn't help smiling.

"Want to take a drive with me?"

"You forget that I've seen you drive. What sort of dimwitted girl do you take me for?" Lovey surprised herself by flirting back.

"Oh, not dimwitted at all. On the contrary, one of the most interesting girls I've met in quite some time."

"Is that so?" Lovey leaned back on outstretched arms, somehow no longer bashful about the damp blouse and skirt clinging to her body like she was sealed up tight in pale blue fabric.

"Absolutely." Royal pulled some saltines and sliced cheese from the basket and laid them out on a gingham print cloth napkin. Then she pulled a small glass bottle out and popped the cork free. She offered the bottle to Lovey.

"What is it?"

"Blackberry cordial. My mother makes it. Mostly for cooking, but I like to drink it sometimes."

Lovey accepted the bottle and took a couple of sips before handing it back to Royal.

"Why were you out driving last night?"

"I run moonshine for my grandfather." Royal took a swig from the bottle.

"Is that so?"

"Yeah, it's sort of my family's side business. Well, truthfully, farming is our side business. Whiskey is a bit more profitable than farming at the moment, given the price of corn." Job opportunities in the rural hill country of north Georgia remained sparse, and income from liquor sales kept families afloat. "Our family has a long history of turning crops into spirits. Apples into brandy and corn into whiskey."

Royal thoughtfully studied Lovey's reaction as she took a cracker with cheese. She reckoned she might as well get the truth out in the open. There was no point in spending time together if the notion of moonshining was going to be a deal breaker. She'd delivered the news, but Royal was having a hard time reading Lovey's expression. Was she surprised? Or was she upset? She didn't seem to be either.

"So that's why you were driving so fast?"

"I was just testing the car and the road. I don't usually drive this way, but Ned thought it might be a quicker route to the Atlanta Highway now that the road's been graded." Royal watched Lovey take another sip, while never breaking eye contact. Royal was paying particular attention to Lovey's mouth on the lip of the green glass bottle, and the distraction caused her to lose her train of thought momentarily. Lovey ran her tongue over her lips, which caused Royal's cheeks to suddenly feel hot. She cleared her throat and looked away. "I guess as long as I coordinate my drives with your late night walks it'll be a safe route."

Lovey laughed softly. "I am sorry about that. But I'm not sorry we met."

She turned back to face Lovey. "Me either."

"So, do you work on cars too or is that Ned's purview?"

"That's all, Ned. I just drive." Royal leaned back on an elbow, feeling oddly relaxed and excited at the same time. "Luckily, I was braking when I came into that curve so I had slowed down before I went into that rollover."

"Is that what you call that upside down move?"

"Yeah, I like to avoid rollovers. At least when I'm behind the wheel of a car."

"So in other instances a rollover might be advantageous?"

Royal didn't think she was imagining it. Something was happening between them. Something unexpected. She couldn't quite figure Lovey out. She was the daughter of a minister. A very conservative Baptist minister. And she'd been married. But unless Royal was way off her game, Lovey was definitely flirting with her. The way Lovey held direct eye contact with her. The way she'd licked her lips just now when she knew Royal was watching. Truth be told, Lovey probably had more experience than she did. She seemed a little bit older and more confident. Maybe Royal was out of her league, but what the hell?

"I can think of a few instances where a rollover is quite nice." Royal took a swig of the tartly sweet cordial and watched Lovey smile slyly back at her. Oh yeah, this was definitely flirtation.

Royal liked the fact that Lovey was taking her at face value. She'd asked hardly any of the usual get-to-know-you questions. She seemed to be interested in coming to her own conclusions. And it seemed like they'd moved past the mention of moonshine without incident.

"Would you go out with me Saturday night?" Royal tried to ask the question with more confidence than she was feeling.

Lovey didn't respond right away, and for a minute Royal thought she'd pushed her luck, but then she answered.

"Yes. I'd like that."

Royal settled back, folding her arms behind her head. Lovey lay down on her side, propped up on one elbow. They were comfortably quiet with each other as they lay in the warm breeze, the smell of grass and damp earth surrounding them. After a minute, Lovey rolled onto her back so that they were lying side by side, inches away but not making contact. Electricity seemed to hum in the space between their bodies. Royal could feel it deep down in her core. She'd only spent a short time with Lovey, but she already knew she had a terrible crush.

"What was your husband's name?" Royal remembered what Lovey had said about losing her husband. She wanted to know more about Lovey's life and the sadness that seemed to register sometimes on her pretty face. Like when Lovey had tucked the quilt around her the night before.

"His name was George."

"Do you miss him?"

"Yes."

Royal couldn't tell from Lovey's voice if she was bothered by the questions or not, so she pushed on. "How did he die?" She watched Lovey take a deep breath and exhale before she spoke.

"The doctors called it pulmonary tuberculosis. Most people call it consumption. Probably because it slowly consumes a person." Lovey was silent for a moment. Royal lay quietly, allowing her to reveal details of her life at her own pace. "It came on him gradually. At first, it seemed like nothing worse than a persistent cold." Royal handed Lovey the bottle. She leaned up a little and took a long pull. "He'd be fatigued in the morning and then run a fever at night. He lost weight and had a cough that bothered him for weeks."

"I'm so sorry." Royal didn't really know what else to say. Lovey sat up, pulling her knees toward her chest. Royal sat up too, mirroring her pose.

"By the time he was coughing up blood, we moved him to a sanitarium outside of Chicago. I was the only one allowed to see him. His breathing was shallow and labored." Royal thought Lovey might start to cry, but she didn't. Tentatively, she reached over and placed a comforting hand on Lovey's back. "You know what question haunts me?" Lovey turned to face her. "Why him and not me?"

"Oh, Lovey," whispered Royal. "You can't think like that."

"I watched over him for months. Do you know what it's like to watch someone slowly suffocate?" A tear spilled over her lashes and slid slowly down her cheek. Then another. "And all I keep thinking is why him and not me? He was so kind, so good. I'm not nearly as worthy of living."

"Don't say that." She pulled at Lovey's arm so that she was forced to look at her. "Hey, things happen that we don't understand. And it has nothing to do with who's more worthy or who deserves something and who doesn't." Royal reached for her trousers, which she'd tossed on the ground nearby, and retrieved a small handkerchief that she handed to Lovey.

"If you tell me it was *God's will* I'm going to get up right now and never speak to you again." Lovey dabbed at her cheeks with a corner of the thin linen cloth.

She supposed that Lovey was sick to her wits' end of hearing that particular platitude given the fact that as the minister's daughter she was probably continually surrounded by well-meaning church folk. Believers always seemed to fall back on that sentiment for some tragedy that made no sense. It hadn't rung any less hollow to Royal upon losing her father suddenly when she was a child, and it no doubt had no healing effect on Lovey either.

Lovey regarded Royal's gentle expression and was extremely sensitive to the press of Royal's open palm against her back.

"That is the last thing I would say to you, Lovey."

Lovey smiled, sniffed, and wiped again at the tears on her

cheeks. "Well, now that's settled maybe we can be friends." She used the word *friend*, but even as she said the word, she felt something much stronger for Royal. A stirring of her insides she wasn't sure she'd ever felt before. An unrequited need so powerful that it seemed outside her ability to control the effect it was having on her body. She fondled the handkerchief between her fingers, rubbing her thumb over the embroidery at the corner; the initials R. D. and what looked like the outline of a car. She couldn't help smiling.

"A car?"

"My mother did the stitching. She says all ladies should keep a clean handkerchief on their person." Royal shifted, possibly feeling a bit bashful about the personal detail the embroidery revealed.

"I think most ladies have flowers, not cars. Your mother must be very understanding."

"I would say she's tolerant. She knows if she put flowers on it I'd never leave the house with it."

They were facing each other now, although their bodies were side by side, knees bent. She became aware of Royal's mouth, darkly tinted by the blackberry cordial. She wanted to kiss Royal. The realization that she wanted to kiss another woman quickened her pulse. She'd ever only kissed George.

Lovey shifted closer, never taking her eyes off Royal's lips. After another moment of hesitation, she leaned into Royal, placing her lips lightly on Royal's. She lingered there, with eyes closed, savoring the soft sensation of their lips pressed together.

If the world was still spinning, she had no sense of it, for in the moment when their lips touched everything in motion seemed to still. Even the birds were silent. She held her breath. The only sound she heard was the pounding of her own heart in her chest like a bass drum.

After a moment, she pulled away, not sure what Royal's reaction might be to the kiss. She'd never kissed a woman before, but she'd wanted to kiss Royal since they'd stood facing each other in her father's kitchen. Royal's face was flushed, maybe from the heat of midday or from the kiss. She was about to apologize for her boldness when Royal closed the space between them and kissed her. The kiss was gentle, but demanding. With the weight of Royal pushing against her, she fell back onto the blanket pulling Royal with her. She held Royal's face in her hands and kissed her deeply, mouths open, tongues touching. She felt Royal's hand drift down her ribs to the outside curve of her hip.

This was nothing more than a first kiss, and yet she was more aroused than she'd ever been in three years of marriage to George. While she'd cared deeply for George and they had even been close friends before marriage, this...this was something else entirely. She had a moment of panic because of the strength of her body's reaction to the kiss and broke away from Royal, breathing hard. She held Royal's face in her hands, and the expression on Royal's face seemed to telegraph the same surprised intensity that she was feeling, an intensity that scared her a little.

"Does this frighten you?" She whispered the question as she gazed into Royal's eyes, attempting to gauge the sincerity she saw there.

"I see you, Lovey Porter. And I am not afraid."

Lovey did feel seen. For the first time in a long time.

She pulled Royal's mouth to hers and they kissed. Time suspended as shadows grew longer around them and a light afternoon breeze danced across their heated skin.

CHAPTER SEVEN

It was late the next evening when Royal finally showed up to retrieve her Ford sedan from Ned's shop. The car was already loaded for a delivery to Forsyth County on the northern outskirts of Atlanta.

"Sorry, I didn't make it over last night." Royal parked her grandfather's old truck beside the weathered barn that doubled as Ned's makeshift garage. "I ended up hanging out for a while."

"I kinda figured you might." Ned slid back the large front door of the barn to reveal the car already headed in the "out" direction. "I went ahead and got this all loaded for you. Dad wanted to talk to you about something, but he got tired of waiting."

Ned's father, Wade, Royal's uncle, was as thick as he was mean. Stout through the chest and neck, he looked more like a boxer than a farmer. Which no one believed he was anyway. He was the sort of fellow who believed that the sun rose just to hear him crow. Royal was more than pleased she'd missed whatever directive Wade Duval had planned to deliver. She tried to spend as little time around him as possible and hated to see the long-term effect his aggressive parenting had had on Ned.

More than once when they were kids she'd seen Wade shove Ned with his boot hard enough to knock him down. She never really believed Ned when he explained away a black eye as a fight at school.

Royal's mother blamed a sharp blow to the head for Wade's antisocial behavior. She said after a bad fall from the barn loft he'd never been the same, but Royal wasn't really buying it. Wade Duval was a bully, plain and simple. A coward. Quick to prey on those he perceived to be less significant in any way.

Wade had married his high school sweetheart, Mary, also his sixth cousin, and even she'd left him once for a week after he struck her. The story went that when Wade showed up at her father's house to retrieve his runaway bride, he was met with a shotgun and a death threat if he ever struck Mary again. Royal always wondered why Mary went back to him. Maybe she was already pregnant with Ned. In any case, Mary never spoke about the incident, so it would remain just one of many family mysteries Royal would never solve.

Royal agreed to keep running liquor as long as her grandfather needed her, but the minute Wade took over the operation, she had decided she was going to leave her post behind the wheel. As much as she liked driving fast cars, she liked dealing with Wade even less. The trade-off wouldn't be worth the emotional duress.

"Do you know what he wanted to tell me?" Royal asked as she threw a satchel into the car and stood in the open door.

"Had something to do with payment I think, but he wouldn't tell me."

"Well, then I'll just be asking the usual price, won't I?" Royal climbed in and cranked the car. "Is this going to 306?" Juke joints usually went by an address rather than a name. She wasn't sure why.

"Yeah, that's the place."

"Why don't you ride with me tonight?" She pulled the door closed and spoke to Ned through the open window. He shifted his stance, moving his weight from one foot to the other. He was not much taller than Royal, with a slim, boyish build. They were close in age, but she somehow seemed older.

"I best not. Pop will be lookin' for me shortly."

"It wouldn't hurt to do what you want to do once in a while, Ned. It would do you good to get out every now and then." She knew it was pointless to encourage him. He was beat down, and more often than not just looking to avoid a fight with his father. Ned's solace was the barn and his engine parts. He was always cooking up some modification or experimental enhancement for Royal to try.

They'd always been close. Like twins separated at birth, or like two halves of the same brain. They made a good team. Most of the time she felt closer to Ned than to her own brother.

"I'll tell Pop you asked after him." He banged his hand lightly on the roof of the car as he stood beside it. "She should run good for you tonight."

"Thanks, Cuz. I owe you one." With that, she waved and pulled out of the barn and onto the road heading south.

The car was heavy-laden and a bit sluggish in the turns. But even as heavy as it was on the straightaways, with the speed, she'd lose her stomach as it topped a few hills, the springs in the undercarriage cushioning the auto as it crested each rise. Royal breezed through Dawsonville, heading southwest. Thoughts of Lovey caused her to lose track of time and forget where she was at one point. She was so lost in reliving their late afternoon kisses from the day before that she'd almost missed the last turn. If she didn't snap out of this lovely Lovey fog, she was going to end up all the way in Atlanta proper, with a load full of corn liquor and too many curious eyes.

She slowed and took the last turn down a darkened dirt road; ramshackle wooden structures lined the lane on each side. She slowed and pulled alongside of the last building, its warm light seeping around the edges of the loosely hung front door and a small side window. Music and voices carried well through the pine board walls. She parked and walked to a back entrance.

Royal knocked twice and someone opened the tiny square hole, shuttered from the inside in the upper half of the door.

"Hey, gotta delivery."

"It's about damn time." Royal heard the bolt slide, and the wide door swung open onto a smoke hazed scene of merriment. A muscled, dark-skinned man held the door ajar.

"Hi, Big Earl, want to help me bring it in?" Royal headed back toward the car as two large fellows followed Earl out to assist with the liquid cargo.

Royal opened the trunk to reveal four wooden crates stuffed with hay and glass jars. Each of them took a crate with Royal grabbing the last one. After carrying the delivery inside, she came back for her satchel and closed the trunk. She accepted a roll of bills and then shoved it into the shoulder satchel that was now strapped across her chest. She'd just accepted Earl's offered hand for a shake when a young woman approached and tugged at Royal's arm.

"Hi, Rose." Royal smiled and allowed herself to be pulled away from Earl's hulking frame. Rose was about Royal's age, her brown skin showing a light sheen of perspiration, no doubt from her exertion on the dance floor. She wore a dress covered with a lavender checked pattern, cinched closely around her tiny waist to accentuate her hips. Rose was a beauty, with dark sparkling eyes that usually hinted at mischief.

"Royal, let's dance...we're celebrating. Ella May got married today."

"Is that what all the noise is about?" The dance floor was crowded with black folks, young and old. Dance clubs were segregated, which seemed silly to Royal. The black joints had the best music. In her line of work, Royal could socialize on both sides of the color line with full acceptance.

Everyone was in full celebratory mode—dancing, clinking glasses, and talking in loud voices. Laughter rang loud and often as Big Earl began to pour drinks from behind the makeshift bar to a small crowd of jovial patrons. The dress ranged from fieldwork clothing, to overalls, to suits and dresses—the latter group most likely part of the wedding party.

As Royal swung Rose around in the midst of the revelers, she caught a glimpse of Ella May and her man dancing a jig. More than one celebrator within arm's length reached out and gave Royal a friendly slap on the back. She hoped it was because they were happy to see her, that they genuinely liked her, and not just because she'd been the one to bring the liquor.

Royal stayed on with Rose and her friends for another hour before she headed back north to the hill country. It was long past midnight when she rounded the bend and traveled in front of Lovey's house. She slowed and considered stopping. Should she?

She hadn't been able to stop thinking of Lovey since she'd left her the previous day. Maybe if she crept close to the house she'd be lucky and Lovey would be feeling as sleepless as she was. Royal eased the Ford sedan off the side of the road just past the driveway, behind some trees and out of sight of the reverend's house. The house stood dark and silent.

Royal had a few small stones in her hand that she tossed at the bedroom window once she was close enough to the house. After three stones, a low wattage bulb came on and a dark figure was outlined against the glass. The window slid open and Royal knew immediately she had the wrong room. *Shit!*

Reverend Edwards leaned out the open window into the darkness, his nightshirt hanging loosely past his waist. Royal had ducked between the shrubs close to the wall just out of his peripheral view. The elderly pastor leaned further, squinting into the dark corners of the yard before he closed the window, and moments later dimmed the lamp.

Dumb. Dumb. Dumb. How did she get the wrong window? She heard muffled voices. Lovey must have gotten up and was now talking with her father. After silence returned, Royal slunk away from the window and started to walk back to where she'd left her car. But she was no more than twenty feet from the house when the sound of a window sliding up caused her to turn. Lovey in her white nightgown practically glowed against the outline of the dark window.

Quickly, Royal trotted back to the house.

"What are you doing?" Lovey whispered.

"I wanted to see you." Royal crouched under the window looking up at Lovey. "I accidentally hit the wrong window."

Lovey covered her mouth to keep from laughing. She silently motioned for Royal to climb into the window, which was two windows down from her father's room. Halfway through the opening, Lovey had to pull Royal by her belt to help her the rest of the way in.

"You're crazy."

"I thought you might be up." Once she righted herself, Royal nervously put her hands in her pockets. The room was dark. Their voices were barely a whisper.

Lovey leaned in, smelling Royal's shirt. "You smell like cigars."

"Hazard of the job, I suppose." Royal watched as Lovey opened the door a little, checked for movement from the hallway, and then silently shut it.

Lovey pulled Royal over to sit on the bed. "I'm glad you stopped by. I couldn't sleep." She pulled her feet up onto the bed and patted the space beside her, an indication for Royal to sit.

Chapter Eight

Now that Royal was in Lovey's bedroom she was a bundle of nerves. In her head she hadn't gotten much past throwing rocks at the window. She hadn't really envisioned what would transpire if Lovey actually invited her in. Even in the dark, barely moonlit room she could see enough detail to know that Lovey was wearing a thin nightgown that revealed the subtle contours of what lay beneath. Her shoulders and arms were bare. As Royal took in these details Lovey reached over and entwined their fingers, which she felt all the way to her toes.

"I should go." Royal started to stand up.

"You just got here."

"I know…I…I just…"

"Come here." Lovey moved across the bed to make more room for Royal. "You must be tired. It's late and you've been driving. Rest with me for a little while."

Royal knew that lying down next to Lovey would be anything but restful. Her nervous system was charged to the max at the moment, and if there'd been more light in the room she was sure Lovey would be able to see how red her cheeks were. But how could she refuse?

"Lie down and talk to me," Lovey whispered. She motioned again for Royal to join her.

Royal stretched out beside Lovey. They lay side by side like coconspirators planning some late night caper.

"Does the cigar smell bother you?"

"No, I rather like it."

"What did you do today?" Royal pulled the pillow up under her head so that she could more fully face Lovey.

"I was at the church, helping prepare meals for shut-ins."

"No kidding?" She thought this sounded like something her mother might do, but not a woman as young as Lovey.

"I'm the minister's daughter. It's politic to assist with efforts in the community. Feeding the infirm is a good thing."

"Oh, I didn't mean any disrespect. I was just surprised is all."

"It was actually nice. Most of the women who brought food to prepare are great to talk with. I've been spending too much time in the house by myself the past few weeks."

They were silent for a couple of minutes. Royal tentatively reached over and caressed Lovey's arm with her fingers.

"I suppose our worlds are very different. Although, I'm told moonshine can be used for many medicinal purposes." Royal made the statement with a straight face, but then they both had to stifle laughs.

"Don't make me laugh. We're supposed to be quiet, remember?" Lovey playfully shoved her in the shoulder. Then they were silent again and the air between them seemed to grow thick with electricity.

"I hear it's also good for bee stings."

"Now I know that's a tall tale. I was hoping you'd forgotten about that."

"Who could forget the whirling dervish in her skivvies running full tilt until she splashed into the pond?"

Lovey grimaced. "I'm so embarrassed."

"You shouldn't be. Even Ned noticed what nice legs you have."

Lovey swatted at Royal's arm playfully.

Royal eased closer and shyly kissed Lovey.

Lovey felt her stomach flip and drop. She shifted into Royal, placing her hand on Royal's face. She felt Royal's hand at the small of her back pulling them closer. She couldn't silence the moan that escaped as their kiss deepened and their bodies pressed more fully against each other.

Royal began to place soft kisses down Lovey's neck and

shoulder. The tension on the shoulder strap of her nightgown lessened and the satin strap drooped off to one side. Royal tentatively slid it further down her arm. The upper curve of her breast now revealed, Royal traced her finger across the sensitive skin as she moved back up to capture Lovey's mouth in another long kiss.

Lovey covered Royal's hand with hers, pressing it into her breast. She wanted to be touched. She arched into Royal's palm, and as they moved against each other the fabric fell further until skin touched skin. Lovey shuddered involuntarily.

"Royal," she whispered.

"Do you want me to stop?"

Lovey didn't speak right away. Her mind wrestled between what she thought she should do and what she wanted to do.

Obviously reading into Lovey's silence, Royal didn't stop. She kissed Lovey's neck and moved down, lightly trailing kisses across the pale skin above her breast. She filled her fingers with the hair at the back of Royal's neck, pulling her mouth more firmly down against her chest. After a few moments of exquisite torture, Lovey finally spoke in a breathy whisper. "Royal, I think we have to stop."

Royal rose up to look Lovey in the face. "What's wrong?"

"Nothing's wrong. Everything's wrong. I just...we shouldn't do this with my father in the house." She caressed Royal's cheek with her fingers. "I'm worried he'll hear us." Royal nodded. It seemed that she understood, although the look on her face was full of desire and her cheeks were hot against Lovey's fingers.

Truthfully, Lovey wasn't sure what she wanted, and part of her was afraid that her father would burst into the room at any moment. But she was also acutely aware that her brain and her body were warring against each other at the moment. She felt equally aroused and confused. But now was not the time to puzzle this out.

"I'll walk you to the door." They got quietly to their feet and began to tiptoe down the hallway toward the kitchen, which led to the front door. Royal was carrying her shoes so as not to make noise.

But as they were just about to walk past the kitchen table, the floor creaked and Lovey jumped at the sound of a door opening behind them. With lightning fast reflexes, she shoved Royal into the pantry just as her father hit the light switch for the kitchen. Lovey turned, blinking against the glowing single bulb.

"Lovey, I thought I heard voices." He was in his nightshirt, with a dressing gown over it. His thinning hair was rumpled on top of his head. He adjusted his wire-rimmed glasses to focus on her.

"I'm sorry if I woke you. I had a bad dream and I needed a glass of water." Lovey moved to the sink and went through the motions of filling a glass. She realized that part about being thirsty wasn't a lie.

"Well, do you want me to make you some hot tea?"

"No, I'm fine, really. No need for you to stay up. I'll just finish my drink and go back to bed."

Inside the pantry, Royal was trying to shrink as small as possible so that she was lost in shadows at the back corner. They'd acted so quickly that the pantry door was ajar, and light from the fixture in the kitchen fell through the opening in a long, rectangular shape that almost exposed her feet. She held her breath, listening to the muffled voices in the kitchen.

Royal's heart was racing for a whole different reason than it had been a few minutes ago. Running moonshine didn't carry near the threat of being found out by Abraham Edwards. She must have been out of her mind to sneak into Lovey's room in the middle of the night. First thing tomorrow she needed to have her head examined.

After a few more moments, she heard Reverend Edwards return to his room. The door shut and the kitchen light clicked off. Royal lingered at the back of the pantry afraid to move until Lovey came to fetch her.

Lovey held her finger to her mouth, a silent signal that they shouldn't talk. She walked Royal to the door and whispered in her ear.

"What time will I see you tomorrow?"

Tomorrow was Saturday. Lovey had already agreed to go out with her. Royal leaned close to whisper, "I'll pick you up at four o'clock. Wear shoes comfortable for walking."

"Okay, see you then." Lovey kissed her on the cheek and ushered her silently out the front door. The brush of Lovey's lips against the outside edge of her ear sent chills down both arms. As she crossed the yard in her sock feet, she felt the heavy dew seeping through.

After a minute, Royal was settled back in the driver's seat of her dark sedan. She leaned back against the seat and sighed, composing lines of poetry in her head.

The flame of desire burns my skin
I welcome the relief only your lips can bring
My body holds a space for you.

CHAPTER NINE

R oyal stretched and rolled over to see the sun streaming through her bedroom window. On the nightstand was a rumpled pile of paper scraps that she pulled into bed with her. She propped herself up on her pillow and sorted through the papers.

Lines of poetry sometimes came to her in short thoughts. She'd scribble them down through the course of the day and night. Sometimes in the full light of day the notes made no sense. An idea she'd thought was genius in the twilight hours would turn out to be rubbish the next morning. Those she crumpled and tossed toward a basket in the corner, only hitting two out of the three.

The phrases she'd written the previous night after seeing Lovey still rang true for her. She tucked them inside a leather wallet on the bedside table, climbed out of bed, and pulled on a shirt and trousers. She fished in the leather satchel hanging on a nearby hook for the wad of bills she'd collected from Big Earl. She shoved the bundle of cash into her loose fitting trousers. Yawning and running a hand through her sleep-sculpted hair, she tottered down the narrow, steep steps that led into the kitchen.

After her window hopping antics the previous night until the wee hours of the morning, Royal had slept in. Sleeping in meant it was around nine in the morning. She was surprised to see Teddy was already seated at the table. Her brother rarely left his pillow on a Saturday before ten. He was usually up late drawing.

Teddy had real talent as an artist, and Royal hoped, given his sensitive nature, that he could follow that path and avoid the family business. Not because she perceived moonshine to be a bad thing, but because Wade was far too rough on the boys. Teddy tried to avoid Wade as much as humanly possible, and Royal agreed with that approach. He was hunched over a cup of coffee; long bangs shielded his eyes so she had to lean low to see his face.

"Are you sick?" Royal poured herself a cup and settled into a chair across from Teddy.

"No, why?"

"It's before ten. You're never up this early. I thought you must be ill. Or maybe you just never went to bed?"

"Oh, yeah, you're hilarious." He pushed a clump of hair off his forehead and took a swig of his coffee.

Royal leaned over to look under the table. Teddy was wearing only one boot. His other foot was shoeless and covered with mud. "Where's your other shoe?"

"Stuck in the mud by the barn. I somehow lost a shoelace yesterday."

"Hmmm," was Royal's only response as she tried not to laugh. "So why is it you're up so early anyway?"

"I'll have you know I was firing up the still."

This was something that Royal's grandfather Duke normally did. He'd usually fire it early, while still almost dark, so that no one could see the smoke. If he'd asked Teddy to do it then something must be wrong. He typically asked Wade, if he didn't do the task himself.

"Why'd he ask you?"

"I dunno. I guess he weren't feelin' well or something."

"You didn't ask him?" Royal found her brother's lack of curiosity annoying.

"He's up at the house. Why don't you go ask him?"

"Maybe I will." Royal stood, refilled her cup, and left Teddy to sleepily sag over his morning brew. She stepped out onto the uneven back porch. The house that she shared with Teddy and their mother needed some work. The back stoop had been missing for more than ten years. At some point, her grandfather found a piece of sandstone tall enough to fill the gap, and that irregular shaped, smooth-surfaced stone had acted as the stoop ever since. *If it ain't broke, don't fix it.* Her granddad's words sounded in her head.

Royal sauntered up the hill toward her grandfather's house. As she drew close, she saw him in a rocker on the long, sheltered front porch.

"Hey," said Royal.

She settled into the rocker next to him. His gray hair, thin on top, was wafting in the breeze. She took a moment to look him over. His clothing was worn almost through as if these were his favorites and he wore them every day. His boots were scuffed and seemed molded to the shape of his feet, turned up just a little at the toe.

"Hey," her grandpa responded without looking at her; he seemed to be studying something along the ridgeline in the distance.

"Teddy said you asked him to fire the still this morning. Are you sick?"

"Nothin' serious. I'm just feeling a mite under the weather. It'll pass." He crossed his legs and reached for a glass of water on the table next to his chair. "It does Teddy good to be called on from time to time anyway."

"Well, I won't disagree with you there. Was I as lazy as him when I was his age?"

Her grandfather snorted a laugh. "Not hardly. You was a wild thing, always into something. Good thing I put you to drivin' so you'd have something to settle your mind on."

Royal had to smile. She felt lucky that her grandfather never once doubted that she could do anything a boy could do. He treated her as an equal, not as some fragile creature to be protected. Maybe part of that was also her own doing. If her family had tried to force her into some preordained stereotypical female role she'd have run off long ago.

Footsteps called Royal's attention away from the soft flannel plaid pattern of her grandfather's shirt that she'd been studying. Her uncle, Wade Duval, rounded the corner of the house. All she'd wanted was a moment to check in with her grandfather. It was too early in the day to deal with Wade's surly self. He would usually not make a show in front of his father. His cowardly way was to be as mean as a snake when no one was around to stop him. Actually, to compare him to a snake was demeaning to snakes, which she felt had gotten a raw deal ever since the Good Book blamed them for tempting Eve.

"You got some cash for me?" Wade propped his broad boot on the edge of the porch and leaned on his knee, looking directly at Royal.

Royal didn't respond, but she pulled the money out of her pocket and handed it to Wade. She finished her coffee while she watched him unroll the bills and count them. Her grandfather remained silent beside her.

Seeming satisfied with what she'd handed him, he turned to leave.

"Hey, I think you forgot something," said Royal.

Wade turned and for a minute looked like he was going to say something. Instead he counted off several bills and handed them back to Royal. She was due two dollars for each bottle she'd delivered as a driving fee. During a week's time, two dollars a bottle really added up. A case would hold twelve half-gallon jars of whiskey, and when she removed the backseat of the car for larger loads she could carry almost twenty-two cases. That was some good money, and she'd been squirreling it away for when she felt like doing something besides driving.

Royal accepted the cash from Wade without getting up. Wade and her grandfather stored the rest of the cash in a collective spot to be divided later among other members of the family who worked the still.

Wade nodded to his father and left. She studied her grandfather's tanned, weathered features for some clue as to how he felt about his only remaining son. His expression was hard to read.

Everyone said that part of the reason for Wade's ill temper was that her father, Roy, had been the favored son. Some swore Royal was the spitting image of her father, Roy. She'd been told that she definitely drove as well as he did. No one would likely ever find out what really caused the accident that took his life.

He'd been alone in the car when it happened. They'd discovered his car upside down in a river ravine. It was unclear if he'd been killed upon impact or drowned. Royal shook her head to dislodge more dark thoughts.

"Why you shakin' your head?"

"No reason." Royal leaned back in her chair. "Doesn't it ever bother you that Wade is so sour all the time?"

"It's just his way. There's nothing to be done about it."

"I worry that his eternal bad mood is gonna run crossways with Boyd Cotton some day and we'll all pay the price for it." Boyd Cotton was the local sheriff, and for a small monthly stipend had agreed to look the other way on delivery days.

"What makes you say that?"

"Just a feeling." But that wasn't the whole truth. Ned had confided to Royal that his father had been complaining about the payment to Boyd, which made her wonder how long he'd actually keep it up. Without the little extra cash incentive each month, she figured Boyd would have little inspiration to aid their cause.

"Wade knows better than to cross Boyd. Whether we like him or not, we need to stay on his good side."

The chair beside her creaked as he stood.

"I'm going down to check the garden. Tomatoes might need to be staked." He stepped off the porch. He had a slight limp as he moved. His left foot had been injured in a cook fire as an infant and never properly healed. A special insert had to be crafted for his boot so that it fit his misshapen foot.

"Do you need help?" Royal asked.

"Nah. I'm sure you got better things to do. You go on now and enjoy your Saturday."

Royal decided breakfast and another cup of coffee sounded good. She headed back down the hill toward her house. At about the halfway point she saw someone walking up the hill from the road. She realized fairly quickly that it was Grace. She had caramel-colored skin, high cheekbones, and her lips curled into a smirk as soon as she caught sight of Royal standing on the path waiting for her.

It looked like she was carrying a plate of something. Royal knew that her breakfast plan had just gotten a heck of a lot better, because no matter what Grace was carrying, it was going to be tastier than what she could fix for herself. Driving was her gift, not cooking.

"Grace Watkins, is that a present for me?" Royal shoved one hand in her pocket. In her other hand, she cradled the empty coffee cup she'd carried from the house.

"It most certainly is not. Is your granddaddy around?" Grace playfully brushed past Royal toward the house at the top of the small rise.

"He just went down to the garden. So I guess I'll have to relieve you of your package there." Royal turned and began to follow Grace. She playfully tugged at Grace's skirt as she followed.

"Royal Duval, you keep your wandering hands to yourself or I won't so much as give you a spoonful of Momma's peach pie." She swatted at Royal's hand, but missed.

"Peach pie! I love me some peach pie for breakfast. Grandpa won't mind."

They let themselves into the house. The screen door banged behind them as they went, and Grace moved around the kitchen gathering a plate and a pie server while Royal settled into a chair at the table. Grace's mother had helped keep house for her grandfather ever since her grandmother had passed away. And every so often she made an extra cake or pie for Grace to bring over on the weekend. Grace had spent a lot of time in this house following her mother around while she cooked and cleaned. She probably felt as at home in this old wood frame house as Royal did.

"You're too good to me, Grace." Royal grinned as Grace handed her a generous serving.

"Too good is right." Grace dropped into a chair across from Royal. "Sam told me you rolled your car."

"Sam talks too much."

"Royal, you need to stop taking chances. Daredevils live short lives, and I want yours to be long." Grace reached over and touched Royal's arm. "Who's gonna aggravate me in my old age if you aren't around?"

"I wasn't taking chances. There was someone standing in the road, and I swerved to miss her." Royal scooped another forkful of pie into her mouth. Good Lord, Mrs. Watkins could cook. The sweet fruit filling practically melted in her mouth, and the crust was flaky perfection.

"I heard. Lovey Porter, resident bee charmer."

"For Pete's sake, does Sam tell you every little thing?"

"Sam and I have no secrets."

"I can see that."

"Nor should we." Grace crossed her arms in front of her chest and gave Royal a *you best behave* look.

"I'll keep that in mind next time I think he can keep a secret. I might as well just tell you my own damn self."

"As if you have any deep dark secrets that I don't already know, Royal Duval. Such a big talker you are."

Royal scraped the last crumbs of crust onto her fork. "Man, that was good."

"I guess so. You hardly took a breath."

"What I'll never know is how you stay so thin while eatin' your momma's cooking all these years." Royal pushed the plate forward and leaned her elbows on the table.

"Worrying about you keeps me thin."

Royal laughed. "Stop worrying about me, Grace. I'm gonna be fine."

"Not if you're planning on spending a lot of time with Miss Lovey."

"What do you mean by that?" Royal felt a knot in her stomach at the mere mention of Lovey in the same sentence with trouble.

"Well, she's her father's daughter ain't she? And he don't like your kind one bit."

"Methodists?"

"Don't make jokes. You know what I mean. Moonshiners." Grace gave Royal a stern look.

"I'll take that under advisement." Royal grinned and held her empty plate out as a clear plea for a second serving.

❖

Lovey checked the clock. It was just a little past the lunch hour. She'd restlessly waited for time to pass the entire day, moving from room to room dusting, cleaning, rearranging, settling to read for a little while, and finally now she was kneeling in front of an old hope chest tucked in a corner of the spare bedroom.

She lifted the heavy lid and pushed the hinge into the locked position so that it would remain open. She couldn't remember the last time she'd visited her mother's things. A black-and-white photo rested on top of her mother's wedding dress. Lovey fingered the white detailed stitching on the bodice of the dress and then reached for a linen handkerchief, delicately embroidered with small yellow and pink flowers. Remembering the details of Royal's handkerchief in contrast to the florets made her smile. She replaced the small piece of folded fabric and reached for a silver brush.

Tucked next to the brush were letters written by her father and mailed to her mother while he was away at seminary. The cursive was bold and sure on the front of each ivory envelope, and each one had been neatly undone with a letter opener so that the edges were practically smooth.

Her mother had died while Lovey was still in her teens. Probably the time when a young girl needed her mother most. Influenza had been an indiscriminate killer that winter. Her mother hadn't been the only individual to fall in their community.

There were so many things Lovey still longed to share with her mother. Never would she have the chance to seek her mother's advice about dresses or boys or first kisses or whatever was happening now with Royal.

Lovey's father had tried his best to keep her at home after

her mother's death, but with the demands of pastoring a large congregation, he was too often called away. He'd enrolled Lovey in the Brenau Academy, the only residential, all female college preparatory program in Georgia at the time. When Lovey began attending the academy in ninth grade, she was part of one of its earliest classes, the school having only been established in 1928. She was a year younger than most of the other girls in ninth grade and still mourning the loss of her mother. Lovey found support and friendship in the sisterhood at Brenau. She remained there for college, training to be a teacher. She'd met George at a school mixer with the University of Georgia her sophomore year.

She sat back on her heels, reflecting on her time at Brenau.

Her roommate, Dottie, had ended up becoming her closest friend over the years that they both studied there. They'd seen each other through the tumultuous years of late adolescence and college. Many a night they'd huddled under the covers, cuddled together, discussing friends, crushes, and the events of the day.

Lovey had seen Dottie only sporadically since their graduation. For women, the choices after college were limited, either graduate school or marriage. Since Lovey wasn't from a family of means, she'd chosen marriage. She knew that the congregation had given her father additional support so that she could attend the private school in the first place, for which she'd been very grateful.

Dottie had also married after graduation. Richard was a classmate of George's, so during their courtship they'd double-dated quite a bit. They had a daughter now that Lovey had not even met. With George's decline and illness, Lovey had been unable to visit Dottie after the birth. She felt the sudden urge to write her a letter. It had been too long, and it would probably do her some good to reach out to such an old and dear friend. Richard had accepted a job in Charlotte, North Carolina. He was a banker, and the last time she'd heard from Dottie, was doing quite well in his job.

Lovey closed the lid of the large walnut chest and stretched out across the bed, looking at the ceiling. She'd felt so different since she and Royal had kissed, almost as if she was a little outside her own body, looking back at herself. This afternoon she would see

Royal again, and the anticipation was making her stomach twitch into knots of nervousness. What was happening to her? She was becoming a creature she hardly recognized. She fondled the locket that had once belonged to her mother, which now hung around her neck. She unhooked the chain and laid it on the bedside table.

She rolled off the large four-poster bed where she'd tucked Royal under her grandmother's handmade quilt and headed to the bath for a good soak. It took a little effort to ready the bath before she settled into the tall-sided claw foot tub. The gauzy fabric of the curtain in the window nearby fluffed softly in the warm, early afternoon breeze, and the call of a blue jay caught her attention. The only other sound in the large quiet house was the intermittent drip from the faucet at the end of the tub near her feet.

Lovey rubbed soap over the curve of her stomach and up over her breasts, slowly stroking her nipples. She closed her eyes, imagining that the touch on her delicate skin was Royal's. She groaned and sank further into the tub at the very thought of Royal's hands on her naked flesh. Such a thought surprised her, and she felt her cheeks flame hotly. She was sure she was blushing.

And then she was struck by a surprisingly unpleasant thought. She sloshed quickly upright in the tub, her senses on high alert. What if her father came home early and she had to explain why Royal, the most boyish looking woman she'd ever known, was picking her up on a Saturday afternoon? Surely this would strike him as odd. Lovey was annoyed at herself for not anticipating such an encounter sooner. Why hadn't she planned to meet Royal in some neutral spot, away from father's judgmental view?

What had her father said? He'd be away most of the day. If she was lucky, *most of the day* meant well after four o'clock.

Lovey decided to finish her bath and get ready. In the event that Royal was early, she didn't want to be responsible for any excuse to delay their departure.

CHAPTER TEN

Reverend Edwards had not returned home by the time Royal picked Lovey up for their afternoon outing. Lovey had been instructed by Royal to wear shoes she could walk in so Lovey could only assume they weren't going anywhere too fancy. And even if they'd wanted to she wasn't sure there was anywhere elegant to go locally. That sort of evening would require a sixty-mile drive to Atlanta, the nearest city.

They drove for about twenty minutes from Lovey's house and pulled off and parked along a dirt road. Royal had packed some things in a knapsack, and they were now headed up a sloping footpath surrounded by mixed hardwoods. The temperature would spike and then recede every time they stepped from sun to shade along the trail. In certain spots the trail passed through thick carpets of lush ferns. The walk was gorgeous. Lovey realized she'd been close to this natural beauty but just had not had the energy or the inclination to venture into the woods on her own. Plus, she didn't really know where they were going. The route seemed familiar to Royal, and a few times along the way she stopped and pointed out details. Like an ancient fencerow, partially swallowed up by the understory. Or she'd point to where an old home place had once stood, usually marked by a pile of granite stones that had at one time been a chimney.

As they walked farther, the path began to zigzag, cutting back and forth across the steep grade so as to make the climb easier for whoever might be traveling this way. At one point there were some large boulders they needed to navigate. Royal stepped up first and then reached back for Lovey's hand. It was the first time they'd touched each other since their outing began, and even that small physical connection between them sent a warm electric surge throughout Lovey's entire body. The sensation was so sudden and so strong that she almost stumbled.

"Are you okay?" Royal held her hand firmly as she looked down from her elevated perch.

"Yes, sorry, my foot just slipped." Lovey felt silly that Royal had such a strong effect on her. "Where is this place you're taking me?"

"It's called Church Rock."

"Why? Because people pray that they'll reach it?" Lovey was breathing hard. The last few switchbacks had been even steeper. Royal laughed.

"No, it's because ministers used to preach up here."

"Seriously?"

"Yeah, but I guess they started to lose too many parishioners along the trail due to the climb. Not enough souls made it to the top to be saved."

"You're making that up." Lovey accepted Royal's hand again as they climbed over a few more rocks.

"No, that's a true story."

Royal grinned at Lovey in such a way that Lovey wasn't completely sure it was a true story, but Royal was so damned adorable when she smiled that Lovey forgot to care about the climb. And in a few moments the trail emptied out onto a large granite outcropping that overlooked the entire valley. The view was so captivating that Lovey had to lean against Royal to steady herself and catch her breath.

"Oh, Royal, it's beautiful here." She felt Royal's arm slide around her waist.

"Just like you," whispered Royal.

Lovey turned to see that while her attention had been captured by the view, all of Royal's attention was focused on her. She leaned into Royal until their lips met. After a moment, Lovey pulled away.

She realized they were in the wide open and that anyone could walk up at any time and find them kissing.

"Don't worry. No one is going to see us here." Royal spoke with the tone of sincere concern in her voice, as if reading Lovey's mind.

Lovey smiled and kissed Royal lightly on the lips before turning to breathe in the view again. She hugged herself and inhaled deeply. A few small puffs of white clouds drifted overhead, and row after row of blue-ridged mountains extended as far as she could see. Behind her, she heard Royal rustling through the bag she'd brought with them.

Royal settled onto the rock and pulled food and two colas in glass bottles out of her pack. She hadn't brought a blanket this time, but she did have a couple of cloth napkins. She'd made them sandwiches and brought one serving of Mrs. Watkins's peach pie in a glass container. She'd eaten two pieces of pie and stolen one more for their picnic before her grandfather even got to sample it.

She watched Lovey take in the view for a few more moments before sitting down beside her on the rock. Lovey smiled as she saw what Royal had prepared for them.

"This is really fun, Royal. Thank you."

"You're welcome." Royal offered one of the sandwiches to Lovey and then took a bite from hers. They sat quietly eating and absorbing the bounty of nature all around them.

After lingering long enough to let their lunch settle, they started to walk back down to where they'd left the car. It was nearly six in the evening and the shadows were lengthening all around them. The sun having dropped low in the sky darkened the ridgeline above them as if cutting the world in half. Dark and light.

Royal loved this time of day. Twilight. The magical space between day and night.

As they entered a thick grove of trees, Royal reached for Lovey's hand and pulled her to a stop.

"Sometimes when I'm in the woods at this time of day, I feel at any moment I might stumble upon something miraculous. Something I have long looked for without knowing that I was searching for it." Royal pulled Lovey close. "Or someone I didn't know I was searching for," she added in a whisper. They were pressed together, every part of their bodies touching in the deepening shadows of the heavy canopy above them, the thick, tall trees like a cathedral surrounding them.

Lovey felt Royal's hands slowly move down her ribs to her hips. Royal applied gentle pressure pulling them closer, but Lovey felt herself resist. She was struggling to understand her attraction to Royal. She felt an intense physical tug that she was at a loss to explain, having never been with a woman before in this way. Why now? Why Royal?

She relinquished and sank into Royal as they began to kiss. They moved against each other. One of Royal's hands dropped lower still and pulled Lovey more tightly against her.

The pounding of her own heart filled her ears, and she knew she couldn't stand this exquisite torture any longer. Their lips separated and Lovey whispered against Royal's cheek. "Where can we go to be alone together?"

"I have a place." Royal kissed Lovey for a few minutes longer before breaking away and pulling Lovey toward the car.

They drove back toward the town square. Main Street weaved around a central courthouse and then Royal took the second right and parked near a tailor's shop, a two-story brick building that seemed to have a separate side entrance. Once they were inside the side door, they climbed stairs to a second floor with a long hallway. Doors every so often on either side lined the hall. They had hardly talked on the drive, and Lovey was a bundle of nerves because of her own suggestion to be alone with Royal.

They stopped in front of a door midway down the long hall, and Royal produced a key that allowed them entrance. She held the door for Lovey.

"What is this place?" Lovey asked. She stepped inside and quickly took in the simple fixtures of the room. A washbasin along one wall, a small table set with a typewriter and nearly covered with loose-leaf papers, a bed, a nightstand, a lamp, and an upholstered chair featuring some worn nondescript pattern. She turned around as she heard the door close quietly behind them.

"Remember when I said I had a place I go sometimes? This is the place." Royal dropped the knapsack on the floor and her keys on the table. "The second story is all rooms for rent, and I keep this place for when I need time away. Or time alone."

Lovey walked over to the table, curious about the typewriter and papers. She read the text on one of the pages.

Peering inside one of the relic's former windows
She tried to imagine what things it must have known, what
*   life it carried.*

She looked up to study Royal's face before she slid the paper aside and read the words scribbled on the page underneath.

Of a life lived in the spaces between
A hollow of shadows
Like the space in my chest that aches with yearning
For a place of belonging.

"Who wrote these?"

"I wrote them. They aren't finished yet." Royal crossed her arms and shifted her stance. She seemed self-conscious.

"You write poetry?"

"Yes."

"And you drive fast cars?"

"Yes."

"Royal Duval, the daredevil poet." Lovey held the papers in her hands as she turned to face Royal, who laughed softly.

"Yes, I suppose that's as good a description as any."

Lovey felt Royal watching her as she read more of what she'd discovered. This added a new dimension to who Royal was, and Lovey now realized she was in terrible danger of falling for her. If she hadn't already suspected it based on the chemical reaction that seemed to take place every time they touched, then finding out Royal wrote poetry would have certainly tipped the scales even further.

"Royal, these are really good. You've got real talent." She looked up from what she was reading to see a sheepish look on Royal's face. "Have these been published?"

"I've never submitted anything." Royal's voice was barely above a whisper.

"You'll drive a hundred miles an hour down a winding road at night, but you won't submit your poems for publication?" Lovey set the papers back on the table surface but allowed her fingertips to keep light contact with them.

"The words, they mean something to me. They're too personal."

Lovey reached for Royal, entwining the fingers of one hand with hers and then brushing her cheek tenderly with the other. "Thank you for sharing them with me," she whispered.

CHAPTER ELEVEN

Royal released Lovey's hand and slid the straps of her suspenders slowly off her shoulders. The straps drooped to hang next to her thighs as she pulled her shirttail loose from her trousers, then unhurriedly began to unbutton her white shirt before tossing it across a nearby chair. Lovey watched the entire tantalizing display with rapt attention, her throat suddenly dry.

She had not spoken in the last few minutes, but Lovey felt Royal communicating volumes with the steamy look of desire that darkened her blue eyes. Lovey exhaled softly as Royal moved toward her. She took a step back, bumping up against the table's edge.

Royal was still wearing the thin, tank style undershirt that she'd had on beneath her long-sleeved shirt. The tight-fitting garment hugged the contours of her small, firm breasts and flat torso.

Royal didn't touch Lovey. Instead she stood very close. They were so close that Lovey could feel the heat coming off Royal's skin.

"You smell really good." Royal whispered the words with her eyes closed.

"Are you trying to seduce me, Royal Duval?"

"Maybe. Or should we call this an exploration?"

If this were an *exploration* then Lovey wasn't certain she could survive an actual seduction. Her heart was thumping in her chest. She knew her cheeks must be flushed from the increased blood flow, and she was feeling other things. Things in places she'd never felt them before. Her eyes were closed but flew open when she felt Royal's touch.

Royal's gaze was focused on the fingertip that she was using to lightly trace Lovey's jawline, down the outside curve of her neck and then across her collarbone. She repeated the route on the other side, but this time she was looking directly into Lovey's eyes as she followed the same path with her fingers. The room was warm, despite air circulating from an open window. Lovey could see the slightest sheen of perspiration along the crest of Royal's shoulders.

Royal moved her fingertips up and slowly swept them over Lovey's lips.

Hesitation. For a moment, time seemed suspended.

Royal lightly placed her lips on Lovey's. As she deepened the kiss between them Lovey felt the weight of Royal press against her. Royal kept her palms pressed against the small of Lovey's back.

Lovey was unsure what to do with her hands. Tentatively, she placed them at Royal's waist, and then as the kiss continued to intensify, she fisted the light fabric of Royal's undershirt, pulling it free from her trousers so that she could feel the smooth skin underneath. She felt Royal inhale sharply against her mouth.

What now? Lovey had no idea. She was completely under Royal's spell at this point, barely keeping her feet on the floor. It was as if the room had dropped away and the two of them were floating above a dark, inviting abyss.

She felt Royal pull her into the center of the room. Her bones had softened to the point she wasn't sure she could keep standing, let alone walk. Royal released her mouth and moved behind her. Lovey opened her eyes just as Royal tossed the undershirt to the chair where her other shirt lay. Lovey realized that Royal was now wearing only the trousers, and her heart rate spiked despite the fact that she couldn't actually see Royal in this state of partial undress. She was about to turn around when she felt Royal step close behind her and begin to unzip her dress. As Royal pushed the fabric apart to reveal the slip underneath, she kissed the back of Lovey's neck and then her shoulders, sending chills down Lovey's arms. Once the dress had been pushed off her shoulders and down to her waist, the slip was next. Royal kissed her shoulders as she slipped the narrow satin strap off to the side and swept it down her arms. Lovey pulled her arms free from the top of her dress and the slip that was gathered at her hips. She reached behind, over her shoulder, she placed her hand at the back of Royal's head, pulling her lips against her neck again. She felt Royal's firm nipples against the bare skin of her back and shuddered.

The place between her legs throbbed as she felt Royal's arms encircle her waist and Royal's strong hands move up her stomach to cover her small aching breasts. Lovey collapsed against Royal as she felt her tease and massage each breast through her bra, causing the need deep in her center to increase.

"I'm not sure how much more of this exploration I can stand," said Lovey.

She felt sure she could feel Royal's lips curve into a smile against her bare shoulder. "Me either."

Lovey reached behind her to unclasp the bra and then tossed it onto the chair with Royal's shirt. Royal's mouth was hot against her neck. She covered Royal's hands with hers as they covered her breasts.

Temptation. Lovey had heard her father speak of it from the pulpit numerous times and never fully understood it until now. The vices that seemed to tempt others beyond their ability to resist things like cards or whiskey had never held any sway over her, so she'd wrongly assumed that temptation was a problem for others. No one warned her that temptation would smell this incredibly good, feel so exquisitely satisfying, or burn as hotly across her tender flesh as this did.

As Royal caressed her with the lightest of touches, Lovey visualized herself in the Garden, naked before God. She was standing under the tree of knowledge, looking up into its laden branches, and she knew with certainty the only fruit she wanted to taste was Royal. She wanted to feel the sweetness of it on her tongue, feel the weight of it in her hand. As Royal traced the outside edge of her arm with tender fingertips, Lovey was struck full in the chest by the knowledge that the one forbidden thing was the one thing she desired most.

Royal moved in front of her. Lovey placed her hands lightly on Royal's chest. She was as hot and flushed as Lovey felt. Her hair was somewhat tousled from Lovey's grasping at it when she'd been standing behind her. Lovey kept her hand lightly on Royal's shoulder for balance as Royal knelt in front of her. She unbuckled Lovey's shoes and set them aside, then pushed the dress and slip slowly over her hips, allowing it to pool around Lovey's ankles so that she could step out of it. Royal stood and pulled Lovey into her arms, kissing her tenderly as she caressed her back with her hands.

Wearing only her panties, Lovey became overwhelmed with tactile sensations. Her bare breasts against Royal's, her naked thighs brushed against the rough fabric of Royal's trousers.

Royal moved them toward the iron frame bed without breaking the kiss. Lovey slid into a seated position on the edge of the bed once she felt it hit the back of her knees. Royal took a step back to remove her boots and pants. She wore boys' loose-style shorts under her pants. And somehow, Lovey thought, Royal made the simple boxy undergarment look incredibly sexy.

Royal moved close to Lovey, standing between her legs as she sat on the edge of the bed. They stayed that way for an extended moment as if Royal were giving her space to either stop what they were doing or make the next move.

Unsure of what to do or say, Lovey let her intuition and desire guide her. She pulled Royal's firm stomach toward her mouth and began kissing her there. Emboldened, she slipped her fingers under the waistband of the shorts and pushed them slowly over Royal's slim hips. Now she was at a loss as to what to do next. She looked up at Royal with questions in her eyes.

Royal smiled at her, then bent to capture Lovey's mouth. She eased her back farther onto the bed and settled down next to her. She pulled a light sheet up over them so that Lovey wouldn't feel so exposed. As she lay beside Lovey, propped up on her elbow, Royal again traced the contours of her neck and shoulders, smiling and every now and then placing soft kisses on Lovey's lips.

"Is this okay?" Royal worried she'd taken things too far.

"Yes."

"Can we get rid of these?" She slipped her fingers under the waistband of Lovey's panties. Lovey nodded her assent.

Once the last bit of clothing that separated them was gone, Royal rolled on top of Lovey, pushing one thigh between her legs. She began kissing Lovey softly on the cheek, on her forehead, on her mouth.

"You feel incredible," Royal said. She slid down and took Lovey's tender breast in her mouth.

"So do you." Lovey whispered the words against Royal's ear.

Royal's senses were on fire. She had some vague notion that she should hold back a little with Lovey. She'd been down this road with straight women before, and things always ended with heartache for her, but this felt different somehow, and so she ignored her fears. She was, after all, catastrophically optimistic.

Lovey was so beautiful. Her skin like pliant porcelain, perfect, smooth, responsive. Royal moved her hand down and across the slight curve of Lovey's stomach to the place between her legs. She watched Lovey's face intently for some signal that she should stop, but Lovey only pulled her down into a fierce kiss, raising her hips to meet Royal's rhythmic caress.

Lovey thought she might pass out from the sheer pleasure of Royal's touch. Her strong fingers stroked and circled, building pressure deep in her core until she felt Royal push inside. She gasped at the sensation, her mouth open against Royal's neck.

Royal kissed her forehead and moved down the length of her body, feathering kisses along the way, all the while slowly thrusting in and out. Lovey felt the climax building with force. She reached over her head to grasp the wrought iron spokes of the headboard in both hands as she felt Royal's mouth in addition to her fingers between her legs. Royal slipped her shoulder under Lovey's thigh and began stroking Lovey with her tongue as she continued teasing thrusts with her fingers.

Lovey was coming undone. She rocked against Royal's mouth and let go of the headboard with one hand so that she could fist Royal's hair.

"Oh, God, Royal, don't stop. Don't stop. Oh…" She cried out as she writhed underneath Royal, the orgasm ripping through her body like a lightning strike. She pulled Royal up and desperately kissed her, holding her tightly against her shuddering body.

Had she ever had an orgasm before? Now she wasn't sure. She'd definitely never felt anything as intense as this. Royal's hair was damp as she moved it away from her forehead and kissed her. She pushed Royal over onto her back and settled on top of her. She rested her head in the center of Royal's chest, listening to Royal's rapid heartbeat. Lovey smiled at the comforting sensation.

Still aroused, Lovey began to kiss Royal's torso and then moved up to her neck, the tender spot under her ear, before capturing her lips in a languorous kiss. She felt Royal's hands drift to cover her ass, pulling Lovey tightly against her midsection.

Lovey propped herself up on an elbow so that she could run her fingertips over Royal's warm mouth. As her fingers made a second sweep across her lips, Royal sucked two fingers inside. The sensation of having her fingers in Royal's mouth sent an electric jolt straight to her core. She felt she understood Royal's message.

Lovey slowly trailed her damp fingers down the center of Royal's body until she could reach between them and stroke Royal's sex.

"Lovey…" Royal's eyes closed as she moved against Lovey's hand. She flipped Lovey over onto her back, straddling Lovey's thigh. Lovey started to move her hand, but Royal covered her hand, holding it in place. "Don't stop," Royal said.

Lovey pushed inside Royal as she moved against her hand and thigh. It was only a matter of moments before Royal tensed in climax and then collapsed.

Lovey tenderly stroked Royal's back as they lay together, spent and breathless.

Chapter Twelve

Royal wasn't sure how long she lay next to Lovey. The sun was long gone and they had not turned on a light. The only illumination in the room came from the moon through the open window. The lunar glow cast surfaces as translucent. She shifted beside Lovey, not wanting to wake her if she'd dozed off. It was hard to tell if she was sleeping. Lovey's eyes were closed; her long, dark lashes rested on flushed cheeks. Her breathing was slow and even. Royal reached into the bedside cabinet and pulled out a glass. The movement caused Lovey to stir.

"If that's a drink, I'll have some." Lovey shifted onto her side and her eyes fluttered open.

"I have two glasses, but all I have on hand is whiskey." Royal looked over her shoulder as she retrieved the glasses.

"I'll try a little."

Royal poured small amounts of the brown liquor into two glasses from the bottle. She considered for a moment the raw materials that were combined to create whiskey. As separate elements, they were nothing more than produce, but combined and heated, they were intoxicating. That was the way she felt with Lovey. Intoxicated. Something existed between them, something incredibly powerful.

Royal handed a glass to Lovey, who propped herself up on a pillow against the headboard. Royal shifted to the other end of the bed, using the other pillow to lean against the footboard. She faced Lovey as she sipped the liquor. Warmth followed the liquid down her throat and to her chest. Royal had dreamed of finding a love, never dreaming that it could actually happen. Pragmatism fought against the idea of happy ever after, but after these past few encounters with Lovey, she could now visualize a faint horizon of hope. As radiant and sharp as a razor blade, paper thin, but a horizon nonetheless. If she stretched, Royal thought she might even see beyond it, her surge of hopefulness allowing her to look farther than she had before.

It was warm in the room. Each of them was only partially covered by the tousled sheet. Royal reached over and ran her palm over Lovey's smooth, slender exposed leg.

Lovey watched Royal watching her as she took a tentative sip of the whiskey. It burned her throat, but after a couple of tiny sips she decided she rather liked its warming effect. She'd never tasted whiskey before.

In the moonlight she thought Royal was more gorgeous, if that was even possible. She felt like she was adrift in bliss. She never wanted to leave this room. She never wanted to leave this bed. But then she realized it might be later than she suspected, for she had surely lost track of time altogether the moment they'd undressed for each other.

"What time do you think it is?" Lovey asked. She felt bold and sexy in her state of undress. Her body was barely covered by the rumpled top sheet.

"Maybe eight o'clock." Royal shifted off the bed and retrieved a pocket watch from her trousers. "That was a good guess. It's eight fifteen."

Lovey was glad she'd asked because it meant she got to watch Royal's naked body move around the softly lit room. Just the sight of her slender, nude body sent shivers to private places. She couldn't help smiling as Royal returned to her spot at the foot of the bed facing her.

"What's funny?" asked Royal. She took another small sip of whiskey.

"I'd say it's more of a question of who's adorable. You."

Royal crawled up the bed and snuggled next to Lovey and kissed her on the cheek. "Maybe I should take this from you now." Royal reached for Lovey's glass. "It's clearly affecting your vision."

"Hardly. But maybe you should take this away from me anyway. I'm not sure I should have too much. I have no tolerance for alcohol."

"So, you have tasted whiskey before? I thought all you Baptists were teetotalers."

"Most of us are. And no, I haven't tasted this particular liquor before. I'm more of a champagne fan. I tried some a few times with friends in Chicago."

"What was Chicago like?" Royal set the two glasses on the nightstand and settled farther down on the pillow so that their bare shoulders were touching. She pulled Lovey's fingers to her lips and kissed them.

"Chicago was magical. Like your lips against my skin." Lovey leaned over and kissed Royal softly. The taste of whiskey still on her tongue mingled with the flavor that Lovey was beginning to recognize was all Royal.

They kissed for a few minutes and snuggled closer together. Lovey slid her thigh over Royal's and snuggled into her neck. "I should go soon," said Lovey.

"How much time do we have?" Royal pulled Lovey closer.

"Enough."

CHAPTER THIRTEEN

It was almost ten by the time Royal dropped Lovey back at her house. It took everything Lovey had to pull herself out of the car, away from Royal, and go inside to face her father. She'd been devising a cover story for her outing during the drive home. She knew she would not be able to exist with Royal in this private bubble forever, but she hoped to make it last as long as possible.

Her father was in his study. The door was ajar as she walked down the hall toward her room.

"Lovey? How was your evening?" He called through the open door. He was at his desk, surrounded by open books and papers.

"It was nice." Lovey leaned on the door frame of his study for a moment. "I'm tired. I think I'll turn in."

"Okay, see you in the morning."

"Good night." She'd avoided questions for the moment, but as she settled into her nightgown in her room she knew that the questions would eventually come. Who had she been with? Where had they gone? What had they done?

What have I done? Sensations of her time with Royal washed over her like a rogue wave. Feeling unstable and a little light-headed, she crawled under the covers and pulled a pillow to her chest.

Creeping sadness swallowed her up like quicksand. The more she tried to redirect her thoughts to struggle against it, the deeper she sank. What did it matter if she'd discovered the most wonderful thing in the world if society wouldn't allow it to exist? She knew her father would disown her if he ever found out she was involved with a woman.

Maybe if Royal dressed or looked in such a way that she could blend in. Would that make a difference? No. Part of what Lovey found so attractive about Royal was her disdain for convention. She knew this, and at the same time she feared it. For all her elevated discourse about women's roles and modernity, deep down she knew the conservatism she'd been raised in had deep sunk roots. Until she could fully exorcise those deeply ingrained origins she would never be truly free. She was afraid she wasn't brave enough to exist openly with Royal.

Even as she thought these things, even as she mourned the loss of what could never be, she started planning a way to be alone with Royal again. Even though part of her psyche knew she was setting herself up for heartache by doing so.

❖

Lovey held the coffee cup in both hands and sipped. Her father sat across from her, coffee in hand, reading over his notes.

"So, who were you with last night?" He asked the question without looking up.

"Just a friend from church. What is your topic for the service this morning?" Lovey usually liked to hear her father talk about his chosen message. She felt a certain sense of specialness getting to hear the raw message before anyone else. However, this morning her agenda was to distract him away from his questions about how she'd spent the previous evening, or with whom.

"Service of others."

"Sounds promising." Lovey watched him pore over his notes. She knew he was only half in the room at the moment, practicing his sermon delivery in his head. She watched him stand absently and refill his coffee.

"You should get ready. We'll be late." He spoke to her while his attention remained on the open Bible in his hand. He left the room, carrying his coffee as he turned into his study and pulled the door shut.

Lovey held her head in her hands. She was a grown woman, but at the moment she felt like a teenager attempting to keep some secret from her parent. Shouldn't she be able to spend time with whomever she chose at this point? She rinsed her cup and moved with leaden feet down the hall to bathe and get dressed for church.

When did attending a worship service become such a chore? Was it only because her faith had failed to explain the events of her life? Was that even the role of faith? She'd been taught that God's hand was at work in all things of this world and that believers were to trust in the infallible workings of his deeds. If that were true, if God was at work in all things, then why had this incredibly strong attraction for Royal developed? Was God testing her ability to overcome temptation? If that were the case she'd already failed the test miserably.

What happened to a person's faith when it seemed to have no relevance to their actual life? She had no answers to any of her questions, and the path her mind had taken was doing nothing but increasing her annoyance level.

Lovey pulled a dress from her narrow closet and tossed it onto the bed so that she could begin to get dressed for church.

❖

Lovey sat in her usual spot in the second pew, near the aisle. She schooled her expression so that her face gave the impression of rapt attentiveness, when in reality she was anything but attentive. Her body was at rest, her back firm against the stiff wood; her mind was in bed with Royal. Heat rose to her throat and décolleté as she remembered Royal's hands on her skin.

Stop. Focus. She forced her attention back to her father in the pulpit.

"The more abundantly I love you, the less I be loved. Second Corinthians, chapter twelve, verse fifteen, talks of Paul's willingness to love without thought of reciprocity." Her father paused for effect and shifted from behind the pedestal upon which his Bible rested. "Paul was talking to all of us who claim to be Christian. His challenge was for us to love others so that they may come to know Christ." His voice grew solemn. "Natural love expects something in return, but not Christ's love, not Christian love."

Lovey shifted on the stiff pew. Every time her father said the word *love* she flinched, as if she were taking each utterance of the word personally. As if each time he said it he was looking right through her. As if he somehow knew where her mind had wandered.

"Christ calls us to serve him by serving others. This is his great command."

Lovey's mind drifted during the last part of his sermon. Her foot twitched to be free of this forced stasis. She fanned herself as the air around her seemed to grow thick with the heat she felt sure was emanating from her entire body. The words *closing hymn* called to her through her fog of distraction, and she sighed with relief knowing release was soon at hand.

"Walk in love, as Christ has loved us. Let us turn to page sixty in our hymnals." Her father signaled for the pianist to begin to play. "And let all those who are burdened come and kneel at the altar and I will pray with you." He nodded again at the pianist and she began to play "I Surrender All."

The congregation stood. Some with raised hands swayed and sang the tune from memory with closed eyes. *I surrender all, I surrender all.* The emotion in the room rose to a crescendo as a couple of people came to the front and those closest left their seats to lay hands on those kneeling. "Praise Jesus," was uttered barely above a whisper from those kneeling near the front.

The ballad insinuated itself in the recesses of Lovey's brain. *Now I feel the sacred flame.* Any mention of flame just rocketed her mind back to the heat she'd felt with Royal. Standing as she was, she had to grab hold of the back of the pew in front of her to stabilize herself. How could one encounter have such a lingering, powerful effect on her?

She opened her eyes. Those gathered at the front seemed to

be in a thrall under her father's spell. Lovey marveled at how her father's sermons could move people. Did he really believe his own words? His conviction seemed sincere. Had nothing ever shaken his faith? Even when he sat at the bedside of her mother in her last hours? Lovey wondered why she had never asked him. Maybe she didn't really want to know the answer. Maybe she'd needed to cling to his belief at the time. But after what she'd gone through losing George and now, confronted with feelings for Royal, that some would label unnatural, doubts were rising for her again.

CHAPTER FOURTEEN

After the service, Lovey stood at the fringe of the small crowd as the congregation exited the narrow wooden church. Her father stood at the exit, greeting each parishioner as they left. Lovey smiled politely and shared a word or two with some of the families as they departed. As the crowd thinned, anxious to leave and find some time alone with her thoughts, she was just about to walk to her father's dusty black Model A Ford when she heard his voice behind her.

"Lovey, we've been invited to Sunday dinner." She turned as he stepped near her. The last thing she felt like doing was having lunch with some family she barely knew.

"You know the Dawsons? Joe here has extended the invitation and I've accepted." Her father motioned Joe Dawson over so there was nothing she could do but smile and graciously accept. Joe was near her age, maybe a year or two older. He was handsome in that outdoorsy, farm boy sort of way, tall and fit, with neatly cropped dark hair and brown eyes. Joe had an easy self-confidence about him as he shifted his stance and fingered the felt hat he was holding.

"Hello, Miss Lovey," Joe said. "You look fine today."

"Thank you, Joe." She shielded her eyes from the midday sun as she looked up to meet his gaze.

"Well, then, Joe, we'll be along shortly, I just need to close up the sanctuary."

Joe nodded, replaced his hat, and left them to their tasks.

Lovey was tired and wanted to go home, but there would be no quietude now. They'd be lunching with the Dawson family, and she felt sure that would be an all-afternoon affair.

❖

Lunch with the Dawsons hadn't been as painful as Lovey had feared. The conversation was cordial and easy. The food was very good—fried chicken, mashed potatoes, and fresh green beans, followed by apple cobbler. Joe's mother was obviously a talented cook. Even still, Lovey struggled to remain in the present. Her thoughts were continually drifting to Royal. What was Royal thinking about their time together? Did she also attend church today? Where was Royal having lunch? When would they be able to see each other again? It was during this last rumination that she heard her name, which pulled her back to the moment at hand.

"I'm sorry, what?" She refocused her gaze in Joe's direction.

"I was just asking, if you've finished, would you like to take a walk?"

For a moment she didn't know what to say. She wanted to say no, but that didn't seem like an option, given everyone at the table was waiting for her response. "Oh, thank you, but I should help clear the table since your mother prepared such a fine meal."

"Oh, don't you worry about that, Lovey. Elaine can help me with the dishes. You go on with Joe and have a nice walk." Joe's mother stood and nodded for Joe's younger sister, Elaine, to help her as she reached for an empty dish. Well, that was it. There would be no getting out of it now. How many times in her life had she been called upon to do the right thing, the thing expected of her? And she was required to do it politely, without complaint for her own needs or wishes. Lovey stood, smiled, and thanked Mrs. Dawson for feeding them and then followed Joe outside. Her father and Mr. Dawson moved to the front porch with tall glasses of iced tea. She gave her father one last look over her shoulder as she and Joe struck out across the broad, flat front lawn.

Chapter Fifteen

Each crisp snap echoed in Royal's ears as she sat with the large pan of beans in her lap. She sat cross-legged on the porch breaking the beans into small pieces so that her mother could can them. She'd gotten up early with the notion that she'd get all her chores done and head into town in the hopes of seeing Lovey. And if she didn't happen to bump into her there, she'd already decided to drive out to her house. She ached to see Lovey today.

All day Sunday she'd done nothing but think about their night together, and she was as nervous as a long-tailed cat in a room full of rocking chairs, pensive about how Lovey might be feeling. Was she regretting that they'd slept together? Royal sure hoped not, because she certainly wasn't. But she knew all of this was new to Lovey, and as far as she knew it might just be experimentation on Lovey's part. It didn't feel that way when they were together, but the demands of family could close in on you and push you in other directions. Royal had seen it happen.

Royal had been through that before with women who wanted to be with her, but only until they met the right man. Then they were off to start a family of their own. They were always nice about breaking things off. Mostly, they just didn't take a relationship with a woman seriously. It seemed that it was a placeholder until they found something *real*. The thought of those old hurts gave Royal's stomach a sour turn.

She snapped the last handful of string beans and stirred the large bowl to make sure she'd gotten them all. Then she carried them to the kitchen where her mother was boiling glass jars for canning.

"I'm thinkin' of going into town after I clean up." Royal leaned against the kitchen sink, watching her mother work. "Do you need anything?"

"Check with your grandfather. We might be low on sugar." Even though her mother was rarely directly involved with the still, she did manage to keep abreast of the raw ingredients distilling required.

"Okay, I'll check with him. Is he feeling better? He seemed a little under the weather on Saturday." Royal headed toward the bath at the back of the house.

"I haven't seen him today so I guess when you see him you'll know more than I do." She didn't look up from her task at the stove.

❖

It was well after lunch before Royal made it to the general mercantile in town. Dawsonville was a sleepy town in the summertime. Folks moved slowly in the heat and humidity, not wanting to overexert and ruin their fresh shirts by breaking a sweat rushing about. Ladies fanned themselves as they chatted together on shady benches. Gentlemen gathered on the sheltered porch of the long, low building, smoking and talking. Overalls and white shirts turned up to the elbow were the usual attire. Royal nodded hello as she walked past a small group of men. She knew most of them from her nighttime deliveries.

It took a moment for her eyes to adjust to the dark interior space. The general store stocked almost every item you could think of. Shoes, hats, fishing poles, baskets, and bolts of cloth sat along shelves that ran down the length of the far wall. There was a long counter, part of which was a glass case containing all manner of smaller items. There was a colorful assortment of penny candies, pocketknives, matches, and other sundries. Royal headed toward the back counter, past more shelves stacked with canned goods.

"Hiya, Royal." A stout older fellow behind the counter spoke to Royal as she walked up.

"Hey, Smiley. Could I get two ten-pound bags of sugar and one of those bottled Cokes?" Doug "Smiley" Sims's nickname suited him as he grinned at Royal over the glass case while she fished in her pocket for some cash.

"Comin' right up." He popped the top on the cola he'd lifted out of a cooling bin with ice, and handed it across the counter. "Gonna be a warm one today."

"Yep, matter of fact, it already is." Royal sipped the soda and looked around the expansive, cluttered interior space. It took a minute before she saw Lovey, peeking around a magazine rack at the other side of the store. The bags of sugar forgotten, she headed over.

Once she was within a few feet of Lovey, nerves got the best of her. She shoved her free hand deep into her trouser pocket and rocked back on her heels. "Hey," was all she could manage.

"Hey, yourself." Lovey smiled. Royal couldn't tell if Lovey was the least bit nervous, which only added to her discomfort.

"I was hoping I'd run into you." Royal kept her voice low.

"So was I." Lovey flipped the pages of the magazine in her hand absently. Was she trying to seem nonchalant? Or was she actually that calm? Royal wasn't sure.

"I didn't know how to reach you," Lovey said.

"Yeah, we need to sort that out." Royal offered the cola to Lovey. "Would you like a sip?"

"Sure." Lovey took a long draw from the bottle, never breaking eye contact with Royal as her mouth touched the glass lip. Butterflies the size of hummingbirds were crowding Royal's stomach. Just the sight of Lovey and any attention paid to her red lips was more than Royal's nervous system could apparently tolerate. She needed to figure out a way to get Lovey alone and away from nosy bystanders.

"Here's your sugar, Royal," said Smiley.

"Thank you!" Royal turned back to Lovey. "Can I offer you a ride home?"

Lovey nodded, smiling. She handed the soda back to Royal,

but just as she did, something caught her eye over Royal's shoulder. Royal turned and followed Lovey's gaze. Joe Dawson had just stepped through the front door of the shop.

"That's Joe. Do you know him?"

"Yes, my father and I had lunch with his family yesterday after the Sunday service. I should say hello." Lovey gave Joe a small wave.

"I'll pay for the sugar, then we can go if you're ready."

"Okay."

Lovey moved toward the door. She thought she might get outside with just a friendly wave to Joe when she knew he'd noticed her, but he met up with her halfway across the room. She checked to see that Royal was still at the back counter settling up for the sugar before refocusing her attention on Joe.

"Hi, Lovey. What a nice surprise."

"Hello, Joe. It was nice to eat lunch with your family yesterday. And thank you for the walk after." Joe and Lovey had strolled all around the Dawson farm. Joe had talked nonstop about his plans for the place, which he would inherit at some point as the only son. They had quite a spread. Lovey had learned the county was even named after a Dawson ancestor. He'd stopped and introduced her to each of his quarter horses. He'd been interesting enough, and she'd enjoyed his company, although on the drive home her father seemed a little too interested in what she and Joe had talked about. She suspected he was up to some sort of matchmaking.

Under other circumstances, any girl would be glad to have Joe's attention, even Lovey. But at the moment she was utterly distracted by someone else. Lovey glanced over at Royal again, anxious to end the encounter with Joe and be on her way.

"I was—" they both said at the same time.

"Sorry, you go first," offered Joe with a chuckle.

"No, you."

"Well, I was just gonna ask if I could call on you later this evening? I've got some things to run back to the farm, but I'll be finished around seven."

Lovey was caught off guard, but in an instant she decided it would be in her best interest to accept Joe's invitation. If she wanted to throw her father off her trail so that she could spend some time with Royal, then time with Joe would be the perfect shield.

"Uh, that would be nice." Lovey started moving toward the door.

"Great. I'll see you at seven then." Joe tipped his hat as Lovey brushed past him and out the exit.

She walked slowly toward where she saw Royal's parked car. Royal caught up to her before she reached it.

"Just let me throw this in the back." Royal popped the trunk and tossed the sugar in. Lovey hoped that Royal wouldn't ask any questions about her brief conversation with Joe. To her relief, she didn't.

The first few minutes of the drive, they were quiet. Lovey thought Royal seemed a little nervous, which she found completely endearing. When they'd made love, Royal had seemed so sure of herself, so confident, in contrast to how she was acting at the moment.

Lovey wanted to cross the electrified space between them and touch Royal. Noticing Royal's long fingers clasping the steering wheel tightly reminded her of how amazing those hands felt as they caressed her naked body. The interior of the car suddenly felt twenty degrees warmer. She couldn't stand it any longer. She leaned over and brushed the back of her fingers across Royal's cheek. Royal glanced over at her with a look Lovey couldn't quite decipher. She pressed closer, lightly kissing Royal's neck just beneath her ear.

The car swerved and dropped off the shoulder momentarily before Royal pulled the heavy sedan back onto the road in a cloud of dust.

"I don't think I can drive when you do that." Royal blushed.

"Then maybe we should pull over, because I'm not sure I can stop." Lovey kissed Royal's neck again as she ran her fingers through the short hair at the back of Royal's neck.

They approached a dirt road on the left, and Royal pulled off the main highway. She drove for a couple of minutes so that they were well off the pavement before she pulled the dark auto up under lush hardwoods into the shade.

In less than a minute they were snuggled into the broad backseat of the car kissing. Lovey felt as if she couldn't get close enough to Royal. They were seated beside each other, locked in an embrace, and Lovey moved her leg so that it was almost across Royal's lap. She wanted to be as close as possible as they kissed.

"I was afraid you'd be sorry about what we did the other night," Royal whispered close to her ear.

"What we did just made me want more. More time with you." She felt Royal's lips curl into a smile against her cheek. Then Royal's lips drifted down her neck as she felt Royal unbutton her blouse. She began doing the same to Royal's shirt. She felt Royal's fingers inside her top; lightly teasing fingertips moved across her stomach muscles, which flinched in response.

Lovey wanted Royal's hands under her skirt. The fabric was loose fitting below her waist, so she shifted so that both legs were across Royal's lap, within easy reach. It was only a moment before Royal began to explore Lovey's inner thigh, slowly easing the light cotton fabric of the skirt up her legs as they continued to kiss.

Royal's fingers paused before reaching the aching place between Lovey's legs. Lovey pulled Royal into a deep kiss as a way to signal her consent for what Royal was doing. Lovey had never really considered herself a sexual person, but at the moment she clearly was. She was in the backseat of a car and wanted nothing more than to be completely undressed and under Royal's attentive touch. *Pleasures of the flesh* had taken on new meaning for her.

She wrapped her fingers around Royal's wrist and pushed her hand further against her throbbing center. That small bit of confirmation seemed to be all that Royal needed. She leaned into Lovey and kissed her deeply. Lovey felt Royal's fingers pull the thin satin fabric aside to caress her tender flesh.

"Oh, Royal," she breathed against Royal's mouth. "Royal."

Royal began to thrust slowly in and out with her fingers. As she leaned back against the side of the car, Royal's mouth drifted down to her breast. Lovey pulled the fabric aside to give Royal better access as she filled her fingers with Royal's hair.

After spending nearly forty-eight hours doing little else but thinking of Royal's hands on her again, she climaxed quickly. She arched into Royal as the orgasm washed forcefully over her.

"I can't believe we just did that," she whispered into Royal's hair. Royal's lips were tenderly kissing the contours of her exposed breasts.

"I can. I've been able to think of nothing but you since you left my room Saturday night." Royal raised up a little so that Lovey could see her face. Lovey pushed damp hair off Royal's forehead, that same sexy clump of hair that seemed to be forever covering those piercing blue eyes.

Royal's hand still rested on Lovey's thigh under her skirt as she leaned in and kissed Lovey softly. She trailed her fingertips down the center of Royal's chest, inside her open shirt. As her hand neared the waist of Royal's trousers, she hesitated, but only for a moment before she pressed her mouth firmly against Royal's and began to unfasten her belt and the buttons of her trousers.

Royal felt Lovey's fingertips dip below the waist of her pants as Lovey shifted her position. She'd moved off Royal's lap enough so that she could reach into the front of her trousers. Royal involuntarily moaned softly as Lovey's fingers began to stroke slowly. She deepened their kiss, holding Lovey's face in her hands and giving herself over to Lovey's demanding touch. It was only a moment before she climaxed into Lovey's hand.

She felt Lovey move her hand, but she left it to rest on Royal's stomach, near the opening of her trousers.

Royal wanted to say something, but she was afraid she'd say too much. Her senses felt raw, her feelings too close to the surface. She pulled Lovey's head to her shoulder and kissed her forehead, allowing her lips to linger there. She silently composed lines of poetry in her head.

Standing at the edge of outer darkness
Adrift with secret longings.

Royal knew that making love to a woman was easy. It was what came after that mattered to her. It was what came later that meant something. Would this be different? Would they hide their feelings away? Would they only love each other in secret? She hoped not.

"What are you thinking?" asked Lovey.

Royal didn't want to answer honestly and run through their bliss with the truth like a sharp blade. She wanted to linger in this singular place that only she and Lovey shared. So instead of her fears, she shared a wish.

"I was thinking that I'd like to spend the night with you."

"That would be nice."

"The whole night. I'd like to be able to hold you in my arms all night and feel no urgency to let you go. I'd like to have all night to explore all your beautiful curves and caress all the spots that make you feel cherished."

Lovey looked up and smiled at her. "I believe you might be a hopeless romantic, Royal Duval."

"Would you expect any less from a daredevil poet?"

Lovey laughed as she buttoned her blouse. Royal couldn't help but smile. God, Lovey had a great laugh, throaty and sincere. She had the sort of laugh that could chase any shadow in your heart out into the light.

They'd only been back on the main road for a matter of minutes when Lovey felt Royal touch the brakes. She'd been lost in thought watching the lush summer landscape sweep past the open window, her chin resting on her arm. As she felt their speed decrease she focused on the road ahead of them. A car was headed toward them with flashing headlights.

"Who is it?" Lovey straightened in her seat, feeling nervous, but she wasn't sure exactly why. She'd never been stopped by the authorities before, but this looked like a police car. Had they been speeding and she hadn't noticed? The large dark sedan had a single light mounted on the roof, although at the moment it had not been turned on and she heard no siren.

"It's Boyd Cotton, the local sheriff. I'm pretty sure he wants me to stop." Royal slowed the Ford and eased to the side of the road as the other car pulled diagonally in front of them. Royal didn't get out of the car right away, but Lovey noticed her knuckles were turning white from her clenched grip on the steering wheel.

Lovey and Royal sat quietly as Boyd approached the car. He was a stout man, thick through the middle, wearing a white collared shirt, with sleeves rolled to his elbows and dark pants. He had a heavy belt with a holstered revolver. He pulled his wide brimmed hat low, casting his eyes in shadow, as he got closer. He banged on the roof with his hand.

"Step out of the car, Royal." He stood back away from the door so that she could exit the car.

Royal spoke quietly to Lovey as she pushed the heavy door open. "Don't worry. I'll be right back. And don't get out of the car unless he asks you to."

Lovey nodded. Her stomach clenched. They'd just been fooling around in the car. She was sure her hair was a mess. She hadn't even checked her lipstick, and then she noticed at the last instant a smear of red on Royal's shirt collar. The red smudge might as well have been the scarlet letter, because as Royal stepped along the side of the car it was all Lovey could see. She hoped Boyd Cotton wouldn't notice.

Lovey couldn't clearly make out what Boyd was saying from inside the car, and it was hard to read Royal's body language. She didn't seem to be afraid of this man, but she also wasn't striking a defiant pose.

Royal crossed her arms in front of her chest, then decided to thrust her hands in her pockets in an attempt to seem less defensive. She wasn't sure what Boyd wanted, but she sure as hell wasn't going to stir up trouble with Lovey sitting in the car. She cleared her throat and waited for Boyd to decide to say something. He was leaning against the side of the car with a cocky sideways grin on his face. Then he stopped smiling, straightened up, and took a step closer to Royal. She shifted back a step in response.

"You seen your uncle today?" Boyd was several inches taller than Royal; he tipped forward so that she could see his eyes.

"No, I haven't seen him."

"Don't he just live across the hill from your mom's place and you ain't seen him?"

"I don't make a habit of checking in with Wade unless I have to." Royal didn't like her uncle. She certainly wasn't his keeper.

"Well, Wade's been short lately." Boyd leaned back against the car again, crossing his arms over his chest, resting them over the top of his large belly. "You tell him he best catch up or...well, I wouldn't want there to be any trouble with federal men, if you get my meaning."

"I think I get your meaning."

"That's good. You're smart, Royal." He pulled a toothpick from his pocket and put it in his mouth. "That might just keep you outta trouble."

Boyd tipped his head low and walked around Royal to peer into the shadowed interior of the sedan.

"And who's this in the car with ya?"

"This is Reverend Edwards's daughter, Lovey." Royal thought if Boyd knew of Lovey's connection to the local minister he'd be less likely to say or do something inappropriate. She hoped.

"Miss Edwards?" He leaned into the open window of the sedan, propped on his elbows. He had to push back the brim of the hat so that it didn't bump the top of the window.

"It's actually Mrs. Porter," Lovey answered. She sat ramrod straight in the front seat with her hands folded in her lap. Royal could see her clearly through the windshield.

"Beg your pardon, ma'am?"

"Porter is my married name."

"Oh, yes, I'd forgotten. I'm well acquainted with your father, Mrs. Porter. And I'm sorry for your loss."

Boyd obviously knew more about her than she knew about

him, but she didn't recognize him. Her father must have spoken with this man about her return home. But why would her father share personal family details with a man such as this?

"Well now, does your father know that his daughter is taking her life into her hands accepting a ride from Royal?" He gave Royal a cocky sideways look. "Why, Royal here drives so fast along these mountain roads that most of my deputies prefer to just let her pass. They'd rather let her be on her way than risk their own lives in pursuit."

Lovey didn't respond. She watched Royal through the windshield trying to gauge her reaction to this man that Lovey had been around for less than five minutes and already didn't like, or trust. She'd made mention of a husband because she thought it prudent if this man believed she wasn't alone in the world, unattached, but now she realized he already knew about her husband's death. What else did he know?

"She's been a very conscientious driver while I've been in the car, Sheriff. But thank you for your concern." Lovey tried to keep her voice even, despite the fact that she felt protective anger rising in her chest for Royal.

"She's polite, Royal." He stood and adjusted his hat before he reached over and pulled at her collar near where the lipstick smudge glowered at Lovey through the windshield. "Your taste in women is improving."

Lovey felt her cheeks flame hot as he turned and nodded at her through the open window. "Ladies," he said as he began to walk back toward his car. Before he reached the car, he turned back. "Royal, you tell Wade he better come find me and settle up."

Royal watched Boyd pull away and drive toward town before she climbed back into the car.

"I'm sorry." Royal gave Lovey a pained look.

"Sorry for what?"

"Sorry that you had to be part of that."

"What was that about anyway?"

"I'm not sure. But I'm gonna find out." Royal put the car in gear and pulled back onto the road.

"He noticed the lipstick on your collar." Lovey tugged lightly at the soiled collar of Royal's white shirt.

"Oh, damn. I'm sorry about that too. I hadn't noticed."

"It's okay." And she hoped it would be. But deep down in the pit of her stomach she feared that Boyd Cotton was not someone who kept secrets unless it suited him or unless he benefited from the secret in some way. She was afraid Boyd might hold this secret over her head like the blade of a guillotine.

CHAPTER SIXTEEN

Royal had been so rattled by the encounter with Boyd that she hadn't made plans to see Lovey again. She'd felt bad that Boyd had tainted the afternoon by whatever he was implying. Royal hadn't gone to find Wade either. She was in desperate need of a few minutes alone to sort through her feelings.

After dropping Lovey at her house, she'd driven back into town and was now up in her rented room, seated in front of her typewriter. Papers were scattered in disorderly piles, each with a few lines of text or single words.

Royal rolled a fresh sheet of paper into the Corona and hit the return until she was a quarter way down the blank sheet. She took a sip of whiskey and stared at the white space over the black ribbon as the liquor warmly slid down her throat.

She leaned forward and allowed her fingers to hover over the raised keys for a moment before she began to type. The pressure and the recoil of each keystroke was as soothing to her soul as her mother's embrace. She watched the words slowly reveal themselves, lightly embossed into the previously unblemished sheet.

Sometimes she started with only disconnected words.

Sometimes she began by typing small sets of words, bits of ideas not yet fully formed.

The scarlet hue of virtue.
The slanted, tangled earth.
The insistent heart.

She took another small sip of whiskey before returning her fingers to the keyboard.

Possibility, like a door left slightly ajar.

She thought of nothing and everything at the same time. Her mind hummed with considerations of what might be. She was falling for Lovey. She'd known it the first time they'd kissed. And the more time she spent with Lovey, the more her feelings were confirmed.

Royal leaned forward, her head in her hands, and exhaled a long, slow breath.

Lovey Porter, what have you done to me?

❖

As the seven o'clock hour drew near, Lovey regretted that she'd so quickly agreed to let Joe stop by. Spending a little time with Royal on the drive home had done nothing but confirm her growing feelings. And now she'd put herself in a situation where she was going to have to entertain a male caller, when that was absolutely the last thing she felt like doing. In contrast, her father had been very pleased to hear that Joe was calling on her.

At seven on the dot, Lovey heard Joe's old farm truck turn onto the gravel drive. She'd made lemonade and carried a tray with two glasses out to the generous front porch. Joe smiled and removed his hat as he stepped up. After a brief greeting they settled into rockers, with the lemonade on a small round table between the two chairs. Their talk was polite and cordial, covering topics as riveting as the weather, horses, and planting cycles. Lovey knew on some level that Joe was trying to find topics that would be safe yet friendly, and at the same time she found it hard not to just blurt out some topic that might be considered salacious, but might actually give her some indication of his true character. With Southern men she knew you had to peel several layers of the onion back to get to the heart of what they thought. But tonight she was feeling a little tired and sad. The exploration of Joe's soul would have to wait for another evening, if it happened at all.

They lingered on the porch together under the waning sunlight for an appropriate amount of time, about an hour. Then Joe thanked her for the lemonade and bid her good night. There was an awkward moment as he stood to leave when she thought he might ask her to go on a date or something, but he didn't say anything and she didn't encourage him to.

After she watched the headlights of his old truck retreat and turn onto the main gravel road, she gathered the empty glasses onto the tray and carried them back into the kitchen. Her father was sitting in the dimly lit study, next to the silent radio, with an open book in his hand as she passed by on her way to the sink. Annoyed, Lovey wondered how much of her conversation with Joe her father had listened to through the open door.

"Did you have a nice visit with Joe?" her father asked.

She peeked around the door frame from the warmly lit kitchen. "Yes. Were you listening to our conversation?" She tried to temper her question so that the tone wasn't as accusatory as she'd felt it.

"Only a little. Don't be angry. It's a father's job to worry over his daughter." He shut the book he'd been holding. "A father wants to be sure of the company his daughter keeps."

If only you knew, thought Lovey. "Well, I'm going to bed early to read. Have a good evening, Father."

"Good night, sweetheart," he called after her, but she was already headed down the narrow hallway to her room.

Chapter Seventeen

Royal ejected the sheet of paper from the typewriter, crumpled it, and tossed it across the room. There were several wads of discarded work already there to keep this newest addition company.

Maybe she should go find Ned and do something to get her mind off Lovey. Their shared moments were completely taking over every conscious thought. She'd sort of lost her appetite, she was daydreaming at odd hours, and now she wasn't able to string a decent, complete thought together on paper. She stood abruptly, almost toppling the chair.

Maybe she'd sipped more whiskey than she realized. Her head spun a little, and she figured she'd better lie down for a little while before driving. She was just about to slip out of her shirt and boots when she heard a soft knock at the door.

A young boy stood outside her door as she opened it.

"Mr. Duval wants to see you." The boy was rail thin, his overalls stained at the knees, and his shirt collar frayed from many washings and likely handed down to him from an older brother. Royal recognized the boy. She'd seen him around the town square, but in the moment couldn't call forth his name.

"Mr. Duval junior or senior?" Royal rubbed her eyes in an attempt to clear the fog settled into her gray matter.

"Um, both I think. They was both there at the table down at the Mill."

"All right then. You run on back and tell 'em I'll be along

directly. I just need a minute to collect myself." Royal pushed the door closed as she heard the boy scuttle down the hall toward the stairs.

The watch in her pocket showed nearly ten o'clock. It was later than she'd thought. Sometimes when she was thinking and writing it was as if time sped up. She'd lose hours and not notice their passing as she sat with her thoughts. Royal poured some water into the basin that stood in the corner of the room and splashed her face with cool water. That helped. She toweled off, took some papers from the table, shoved them into her leather satchel, and headed out into the night.

Walking to the Mill seemed like a more judicious plan, given her head was still a bit fuzzy. She'd rolled the Ford once already in the past two weeks; she didn't relish the idea of doing it again.

The night was fully dark. A couple of gas lamps burned at the street corners near the marble courthouse casting an eerie glow in the thick, humid air.

The Mill was a nickname for a drinking spot on the other side of town. It had been a gristmill once, long before she was old enough to pay attention to such things. For as long as she'd been running deliveries for her grandfather, it had been a gathering spot for local men. She usually only stopped there when she either had a case to deliver or she knew her grandfather was inside. As was often the case, because of the way she dressed and the fact that she did what most would consider men's work, the townsfolk treated her a bit differently. Mostly, the men weren't sure sometimes how to behave around her. She acted more like one of the fellas. Women weren't always sure how to respond to Royal's uniqueness either.

She knocked at the heavy door of the Mill, and someone peeked around the edge of the door, hesitating for a moment before stepping aside and allowing Royal entrance.

The interior was dark and heavy with smoke and the smell of tobacco. Royal nodded at a few of the men she knew as she crossed the room toward a table at the back. Small clusters of men stood or sat along the wall; some leaned back at an angle in straight-back chairs. Low voices and indecipherable murmurs surrounded her as she stepped up to the long plank table where her grandfather and her uncle Wade were seated.

Royal scanned the room one more time as she pulled out a chair and sat down.

"Drink?" a buxom woman who was tending to the patrons asked.

"No, thanks, June. Nothin' for me," said Royal.

"Okay, sugah, just let me know if you change your mind." June's round form swept past her as she gathered a few empty glasses onto a scuffed tray.

Royal placed her hands on the table, waiting to find out why she'd been summoned. She hadn't spoken with Wade or her grandfather about the conversation she'd had earlier with Boyd Cotton, and she didn't relish the thought of calling Wade out on it in front of her grandfather.

Her grandfather sat across from Royal. His hat hung on a peg along the wall over his shoulder. He seemed older somehow, and tired. Royal wondered for a moment when he would step aside and hand things over to Wade. Royal watched the dynamic between father and son play out across from her. Wade, always challenging, always demanding attention by being the loudest voice in the room. Insistent that other men respect him, while the senior Duval carried himself as a man who knew he was respected. Men stood up when he entered a room. They sought his counsel. Duke Duval was universally liked and admired, whereas Wade was tolerated.

Wade finally spoke. "Where you been all day?"

"Around." Royal was intentionally vague. She wondered if the sheriff had run across Wade already, in which case Wade likely already knew where she'd been.

"We got a big a delivery tomorrow night. I wanted to make sure you came by the farm early to load up." Her grandfather took a sip of the brown liquor in his glass. "It's a full load. Ned will need to pull the backseat out, so get there early enough to do that."

Royal nodded. "Is that all?"

"Yeah." Her granddad studied her from across the table. "What's the rush? You got somewhere else to be?"

"No, I'm just feelin' a bit beat. I thought I'd head home."

"I'll walk you out." Wade stood up.

Damn. That didn't sound good. He never did anything for the sake of politeness or good manners. He wanted her alone for a minute. Well, she'd already announced she was leaving, so there was nothing to do but stand and allow Wade to follow her to the door.

It took stepping out into the clear night air to realize how poor the air quality had been inside the old mill. Royal stopped a few feet from the door and turned to face her uncle.

"You avoiding me?" Wade stepped close, looking down at her.

Yes. Royal rocked back on her heels. "No." Maybe now was the time to mention her encounter with Boyd Cotton. "The sheriff said you need to pay him a visit."

"What?"

"I ran into Boyd Cotton earlier today and he said that you owed him something."

Wade seemed agitated by the message.

"You paid him, didn't you?" Royal had been having suspicions lately that Wade had been making decisions that he wasn't sharing with her grandfather. The deal had always been that her grandpa paid the local boys to not necessarily look the other way, but at least not try very hard to interfere with their moonshining. Prohibition had gotten repealed a while back, but that didn't mean anyone was ready to pay taxes on home brew. Not by a long shot. As a result, lately, the hills had seen an influx of federal revenue officers, and it only made sense that Boyd and his crew would expect payment now more than ever if they were going to run any sort of interference for the Duval clan. Boyd was probably after a raise to compensate for the extra hassle.

At the same time, she knew Wade to be greedy, and she'd seen him argue more than once with his father over the amount they paid the sheriff and his boys. Royal figured the minute Wade had his way, he'd keep all that payoff cash to himself. She suspected that was already beginning to happen and that's why Boyd wasn't happy.

"Well? Do we owe Boyd or what?"

"Listen, Royal, you drive. That's all you do. And try not to break any glass jars while you're doing it. And then collect the money. That's all you need to worry about." He poked a finger into her chest just below her collarbone for emphasis. "You understand? I'll deal with Boyd."

"No, you won't, Wade. If you start messing things up we'll all be dealing with Boyd and probably worse." The federal boys had no connection to the local community. They'd smash your still, riddle your car with bullets. Hell, she figured they'd shoot your dog just for barking at them.

"You're gonna have to get used to dealin' with me soon enough, Royal. You best come to terms with it. I ain't gonna be runnin' things as loose as Pop does. I can tell you that."

"Well, you're not running anything yet, Wade." She wasn't trying to bait him, but her words got an instant reaction. He grabbed the front of her shirt with both hands, jerking her forward.

"We're gonna come to an understanding, Royal. One of these days—"

"Hey, Royal." She turned to see her friend Frank walking toward the Mill with another fellow that worked at the feed store. His presence caused Wade to drop his hold on Royal. She pulled at her shirt, smoothing the front down with both hands.

"Hiya, Frank. Nice to see you." Royal stepped back from Wade. She could tell he was angry, but whatever message he had been about to deliver had been cut short by the appearance of an audience.

Frank slapped Royal on the shoulder. "Come in and have a drink with us." If Frank had any idea of what he'd interrupted, he showed no sign of it. He turned and nodded in Wade's direction. "Evenin'."

Wade simply nodded in response, his expression dark and angry.

"Thank you, Frank, but I was just headin' out. Another time?" She began walking away from them toward where she'd left her car a few blocks away, near her rented room. Wade made no motion to follow, so she began to relax.

"Sure thing. Catch you later." Frank looked back at her as he pulled at the heavy door of the Mill.

CHAPTER EIGHTEEN

The high curved roof of Royal's Ford offered good visibility along the dark back roads. She kept an eye on the side roads for the sudden appearance of headlights and was equally watchful of any lights that might appear in the rearview mirror. The sedan was heavy on its feet as she snaked along the sixty-mile winding road from Dawsonville to Atlanta for the evening run. It was after midnight, and Ned was in the car with her. Her other passengers were several cases of clear liquid in glass jars where her backseat should have been.

She'd wanted to stop by Lovey's house before making this run, but not with Ned in tow. Pulling out the backseat and loading the car had taken longer than she'd expected, which got her off to a late start. Royal hadn't seen Lovey since the afternoon they'd made out in the backseat. She blushed at the thought of it as she and Ned heaved the heavy broad bench seat out of the car to make room for more liquid cargo.

It seemed particularly dark tonight, the sedan's headlights doing little to illuminate her path, given her speed. Luckily, Royal knew this winding road from memory. She knew every curve and just how fast she could take each, depending on her load and the weather conditions of the road.

"So, have you seen the bee charmer lately?" She heard the joking tone in Ned's voice as he asked.

"Why, as a matter of fact I saw her yesterday."

"And?"

"And nothing. I gave her a ride home. I like her. I'd like to see more of her." Royal downshifted as they came into a sharp turn. "When are you going to get yourself a girl so you can stop askin' about mine?"

"I'm studyin' on it."

"Oh, studyin' on it. Is that your romantic method?" Royal punched Ned's arm. "No wonder you're still single. Well, maybe you'll see someone that catches your eye tonight when we make this delivery. The last time I was in this joint there were some cute girls in the fray."

She was on a fairly long straightaway when she noticed distant headlights behind her. Whoever they were they were coming up fast. It was unlikely that anyone but a federal agent would be on this particular road this time of night. And whoever they were they'd have only one reason to be gaining on her.

Ned sensed her change in mood almost immediately. "What's wrong?"

"Looks like we've got some company. They're coming along pretty fast."

Ned turned in the seat beside her to look.

Royal shifted down into second and then hit the gas again as she came through the curve, pulling the high stick down into third before opening up the V-8 on the short straightaway between the curves. It wasn't until she had weaved through several sharp turns before she could confirm that the other auto was still following her. Whoever they were, they were gaining on her position.

"Yeah, they're definitely up to something. They're still gaining on us."

"What are you gonna do?" Ned's voice sounded fearful. Royal couldn't believe the one night she actually managed to talk Ned into riding along with her they'd run into trouble. He'd be solidly spooked now from future runs.

"Just stay cool. I've got some ideas." Royal checked the encroaching headlights again in the rearview mirror.

She was familiar enough with the road to know that a long,

gentle downhill straightaway was just ahead. She stomped on the accelerator. Ned braced himself with a hand on the dash and one on the roof as the heavy car topped a hill, lifting off the ground just a little as it crested the rise.

The pressure of the increased speed sank Royal's back farther into the seat. The gauge on the dash registered just above eighty miles an hour when she saw the headlights close behind her and heard the first gunshot.

"What the hell?" Ned jerked his head down behind the seat. "They're shootin' at us!"

"No shit! Keep your head down!"

Damn! If they were shooting then they for sure weren't local boys. Another shot sounded loudly as the bullet hit the rear quarter panel and Royal accelerated again. She had reached ninety on the speedometer, but she knew another series of quick turns lay just ahead.

Before she slowed the car down, she reached under the dash and flipped a switch to turn off her brake lights.

Of course, with no advance warning from her brake lights and likely not as much familiarity with the roads in this part of the county, the headlights bounced and flickered indicating that they'd driven straight through the turn and ended up in the ditch.

"Thank you, Ned! Your taillight trick worked like a charm!" She reached over and laid her hand on Ned's chest. "Son, your heart is thumping like a jackrabbit!"

Ned swatted her arm away. "It's not funny. That scared the shit out of me."

Royal gave him a sideways glance. "A little fear is good for the soul, right?"

"Not my soul."

"We'll be home free in another half hour. Drinks on me." Given the terrified look on Ned's face, she figured this would be the last time for a long while that she'd be able to talk him into riding along on one of her delivery runs. The truth was, she'd been scared too.

That had been the closest call she'd had in a long time. And they'd fired on her car, which not only rattled her nerves, it made her angry. She loosened her grip on the large steering wheel and realized that her hands were shaking.

Since when did a little car chase rattle her so badly? She'd been feeling distracted all day with thoughts of Lovey. Maybe she was starting to think she had a future. Having a future was making her rethink risky behavior. Was this what it felt like to have something in your life that mattered? Someone you wanted to come home to? Or was it just because Ned was in the car?

She left her taillights off for a while longer as she hit the gas pedal and rocketed into the dark night.

CHAPTER NINETEEN

Another day had slogged slowly by for Lovey. She'd not seen Royal and had no way to reach her. It seemed that if she was going to see Royal she'd have to take matters into her own hands. It was still early in the day when Lovey decided to walk over to Royal's house. She was curious to see Royal's home. After all, Royal had been to her house more than once, although not in the light of day.

As it turned out, Cal knew where Royal's family lived and so she'd gotten directions. She thought she'd just walk over. She was headed that way when Cal showed up with groceries. Today was one of the days she did laundry and cooked dinner for them.

"Are you sure you should be goin' over there, Miss Lovey?" Cal had a concerned look across her face when Lovey told her of her intentions.

"You think it's bad if I walk over without an invitation?"

"No, it ain't that, Miss Lovey. It's just that, well…"

"I know that the Duvals make moonshine, if that's what worries you." Lovey wasn't sure the reason for Cal's concern. It had to be about the moonshine, given her father's abhorrence of the stuff.

"Well, that, among other things."

"It'll be fine, Cal. And it's a beautiful summer day for a walk." She trusted Cal not to say more to her father than she'd gone for a walk if he asked.

Her father was fairly distracted this week preparing for an

overnight revival that was to start on Friday, culminating with Decoration Day on the church lawn Sunday. At least that's what the locals called it. She'd always heard it referred to as Homecoming, but the event seemed to have the same components—decorating the graves at the church and hosting a large covered dish lunch on the lawn after the Sunday service.

Lovey had a long shot of a plan to spend Friday night with Royal. That had been the last request Royal had made, and this might be a rare opportunity to actually make that happen. But first, she needed to find Royal and reconnect.

It was a three-mile leisurely walk to Royal's place, a cluster of wood-sided structures on a large piece of open property. The three buildings were spread out and punctuated by at least one large barn, a corn crib, and a low chicken coop built of what looked like hand-sawed lumber that Lovey could see from the wooded lane that skirted the property. The first house was painted white but worn in spots. That was the structure she had the clearest view of from the driveway. There was another house up a hill set farther off the road, and she could just make out the roofline of a third house camouflaged by a scattering of hardwoods thick with foliage.

As Lovey drew near the first house, she saw a woman wearing an apron that covered most of a floral shirtwaist and her skirt. She seemed to be spreading corn for a random assortment of free roaming chickens in the front yard. The woman looked up with a questioning gaze as Lovey headed toward her. She knew she was taking a large chance just showing up like this, but she didn't think she could tolerate one more day without seeing Royal.

"Hello." Lovey stopped several feet away and crossed her arms in front of her chest. She felt nervous, but wasn't sure if it was due to the intense once-over the woman was giving her or if it was the anticipation of seeing Royal on her home turf.

"Hello."

"I'm sorry to stop by unannounced, but I was hoping that Royal might be here."

"She is. Can I ask who's callin'?"

"Of, course, sorry. My name is Lovey Porter. I'm a friend of Royal's." Lovey smoothed the sides of her calico broomstick skirt. She felt as if she were under astute inspection.

"It's nice to meet you. I'm Royal's mother. Let me just get her for you." Without further delay, she turned and shouted at an open second-story window. "Royal, you have a visitor!"

The two of them stood in awkward silence for a moment waiting for some sort of response. When none came, the plump, matronly woman yelled again.

"Lillian Royal Duval! I know you can hear me."

Royal's blond head appeared in the open window, her hair mussed. She had a shocked look on her face when she saw Lovey standing next to her mother. She held up her hand. "Just a minute. I'll be right down."

"Why don't you go on in and wait for her in the kitchen?" Royal's mother rested the shallow pan of loose corn on her hip.

"Thank you, Mrs. Duval."

The worn boards of the long front porch creaked as she crossed them and pulled open the screen door. Lovey could see the kitchen through the doorway as she passed through a small living room set around a brick fireplace. The room paneled with board-and-batten-style white pine, darkened from exposure to the sun over time, was well kept and cozy. A brick fireplace with a heavy rough-hewn mantel was along the far wall. Generous throw cushions accented an obviously well loved sofa and leather chair. She paused in the center of the kitchen, not quite sure if she should sit down. The smell of something recently baked hung in the air. A black pan covered with a towel sat on the stovetop. She lifted the corner. Biscuits. She dropped the cloth as she heard footsteps coming down the narrow stairs to her left.

Royal slipped in her sock feet on the last step, almost tumbling to the floor. She righted herself before falling completely and then attempted to recover with a smile.

"Hey." Royal ran her fingers through her mussed hair to try to smooth it back.

"I'm sorry to wake you. I guess I didn't think that you might have been out late."

"It's okay. I'm really glad to see you." Royal stepped closer as she tucked in her shirttail. She'd probably gotten dressed in a hurry.

"Lillian, huh?" Lovey tried not to laugh at the pained expression on Royal's handsome face.

"She uses my full name when she's annoyed with me. Can we pretend you didn't hear that?"

"Lillian is a beautiful name."

"Yes, it is. For someone else." Royal reached for one of the biscuits on the stovetop. She nodded toward the skillet, with the biscuit already in her mouth, offering Lovey one.

"No, thank you."

"Um, I need to get my shoes." Royal turned, about to head back up the stairs. "Would you...would you like to see my room?"

Lovey nodded and followed Royal up the narrow, steep stairs to the second floor. A single bulb hung from a wire in the ceiling at the top of the steps, which opened into a large open room with two smaller bedrooms at each end. Of course Royal's bed was unmade and there were clothes thrown across a straight-backed wooden chair next to a small desk stacked with books and papers. There were more books in small stacks next to the baseboards of the wall on either side of the narrow oak desk.

Royal was looking for her shoes under the far side of the bed. There didn't seem to be anywhere for Lovey to sit except on the bed. But she'd not been invited to do so. Instead she stood clasping her hands in front of her and waited for Royal.

"Do you mind waiting just a quick moment while I go wash up a little?"

Lovey nodded.

Royal slipped past her out of the room and clomped quickly down the stairs in her unlaced shoes. Lovey was happy to have a few minutes alone with Royal's things. She moved slowly around the simply furnished room. On the dresser along the wall facing the desk rested a pocket watch. Lovey picked it up and rubbed her fingers across the engraved pattern on the back of the casing. There was a framed photo, probably Royal's father and mother in their younger years. They were smiling and leaning against a dark Model T Ford. The man's head was tilted back with laughter. Lovey lifted the shirt hanging on the back of the chair and held it to her nose. It smelled like Royal, which made her smile. A book of poetry by Robert Frost was on top of the papers on the desk. Lovey flipped through the pages, not really settling on any one in particular. She moved to the far side of the room and sat on the edge of the bed, running her hand across the pillow that still registered an indention from where Royal had been sleeping.

She realized after a moment that Royal had silently returned and was leaning against the door frame watching her as she rolled the sleeves of her bright white shirt. She gave Lovey a heart-stopping slow smile from across the room. Lovey thought she should stand up, but she was immobilized, her heart pounding in her chest.

"I am really glad you stopped by." Royal walked around the bed. She stopped at the footboard, leaning on the tall post at the corner.

"Do you think your mother knows about us?"

"Well, she knows I like girls, if that's what you mean." Royal shoved her free hand deep into her trouser pocket. "And if we stay up here much longer she might begin to have suspicions about what we're doing."

"So she's a mind reader then?" Lovey stood and stepped close to Royal. A breeze blew the light cotton fabric of the curtain away from the window and stirred the hair around her face.

"Whose mind would she be reading?"

"Mine. Right this minute." Lovey took Royal's suspender between her fingers and slid her hand up and down the length of it slowly.

Royal cleared her throat. Her cheeks grew red, which entertained Lovey. Royal acted so tough but was so easily ruffled by innuendo. Lovey found the juxtaposition of those two details adorable.

"Am I making you nervous?" She fingered the collar of Royal's shirt.

"Um, no."

She's obviously not a good liar was Lovey's quick assessment. That discovery pleased her.

"I'd really like to kiss you," whispered Lovey.

Royal leaned in and their lips met. The kiss was short and sweet, with a promise of more.

"Let's take a walk." Royal took her hand and pulled her toward the stairs.

They passed through the kitchen and out the back door. Royal's car was parked near an aging mimosa tree in full bloom that swayed in the warm breeze dropping flowers on the dark sedan. Lovey's gaze swept across the car as they strolled past. She pulled to a stop when she saw the bullet hole.

"Royal?" Lovey walked toward the back of the car. "What's this?"

Royal followed Lovey's pointing finger.

"A bad shot."

"That's not funny. Is this what I think it is? Is this a bullet hole?" Lovey was trying not to get angry, but it wasn't working.

"I'm sorry. I didn't mean to make a joke. It happens some-times."

"Royal, was someone shooting at your car while you were in it?"

"It happened last night. They got one lucky shot before I lost them." Royal pulled at Lovey's hand. "Come on. Let's walk down to the pond. This is nothing to worry about."

Lovey didn't agree with that statement. She felt a sick twinge in the pit of her stomach. The reality of what Royal did for a living crystallized, and Lovey wasn't happy about it.

"Royal, doesn't that scare you? What if it hadn't been a bad shot?" She tried to look at Royal's face as they walked down a grassy path beside a large shed that housed a tractor and the old truck she'd seen Royal drive the day of the bee sting incident.

"Yeah, to be honest, it did scare me a little. But it's over now and I'm fine. I'm not going to dwell on it. Let's talk about something else."

Lovey wasn't finished with this topic, but she decided not to push Royal at the moment. They continued down the path in silence. The grass grew taller around them and opened into a field that wrapped around the base of a gently sloped hill. After a few more moments, Lovey saw a large pond ahead of them surrounded by hardwoods.

Royal sensed that Lovey was upset. Lovey wouldn't even look at her. She couldn't stand knowing that some action of hers had made Lovey unhappy.

"Please don't be angry with me." Royal stepped in front of Lovey, walking backward. Lovey finally looked up.

"It's hard not to be angry, Royal. Someone was shooting at you. That scares me."

"I promise to be careful. Can you just not think about it anymore right now?" Royal wanted to shift the mood between them. She wanted to feel the closeness between them.

"I'll try not to think about it."

"Maybe I could find a way to distract you." Royal entwined their fingers as they walked side by side toward the large shade trees gathered at the pond's edge.

"Your family's property is beautiful."

"Thanks. We've got forty acres now. My great-grandfather used to have almost a hundred acres, but over time he had to sell some of it off. Before we started in earnest to turn crops into spirits." Royal leaned against the nearest broad tree trunk and pulled Lovey against her. She caressed the contour of Lovey's face delicately with her fingertips before she kissed her forehead, then her cheek, and finally placed a lingering kiss on her lips.

"I have a proposal." Lovey leaned her head against Royal's shoulder as Royal caressed her back.

"Oh yeah? What's that?"

"My father has an overnight revival Friday. I was hoping we could spend the evening together." Lovey pulled back so that Royal could see her face.

"Really? You mean, the whole evening?" Royal tried to temper her excitement at the suggestion that they might spend the night together.

"Well, if you aren't dodging bullets or whatever else you daredevils do."

Royal pulled her into a hug. "It's a date. I'll pick you up for dinner and then we can go to my place in town."

"I was thinking I could make you dinner. Would that be okay? I want you all to myself, not in some public venue."

"Even better." She kissed Lovey again, this time longer, more passionate.

Their bodies were pressed against each other, and it was difficult for Royal not to let her hands drift up and down the gentle slope of Lovey's hips. After another moment, she gave in to the impulse. Lovey wrapped her arms around Royal's neck and deepened the kiss. Royal ached deep inside for Lovey to touch her, be with her, to be cradled in her arms.

They separated slowly. Royal felt weak kneed and suggested they sit down in the shade. Bees hummed in the clover nearby as they settled at the base of the tree. Lovey sat between Royal's legs, leaning against her chest. She pulled Royal's hand into hers and turned it over, caressing it with her fingers.

"Have you been writing lately?"

"I've been feeling a bit distracted for some reason. It's been hard to focus." Lovey pressed her soft lips to Royal's fingers, which Royal felt all the way to her toes.

"What was it that made you start writing? Did you attend college?" Lovey settled her head back under Royal's chin.

"No, I stopped after the tenth grade and started driving for my granddad."

"What about all the books in your room?"

"I love to read. Maybe that's my college. Books." Royal caressed Lovey's shoulders and let her hands drift slowly down Lovey's arms.

"I loved college." Lovey picked a clover and twirled it between her fingers. She had to remind herself that to others it might seem that she'd come from a world of intellectual privilege. And now she was in a region populated only with one-room schoolhouses. "I think you would have enjoyed college."

"Maybe."

"You didn't really answer my question about what made you start writing."

"I'm not sure I can put my finger on any one reason. I've always loved books and I love words. I suppose that sounds strange."

"Not to me. Language is powerful."

"Discovering the perfect word, a word that captures something complex, that makes me feel elated. It makes me feel understood."

Lovey watched Royal's face then prompted her to continue. "Why poetry and not some other style of writing?"

"During the time after my father died I discovered poetry. My grandfather taught me to drive and then gave me one of his dog-eared poetry collections."

"So does your grandfather write also?"

"No, but I discovered as a child that he had this secret love for poetry." Royal caressed Lovey's cheek with her fingers. "He told me that poetry was like bread for the soul."

"That's a lovely way to think about it."

"A thoughtfully crafted poem can speak to our deepest selves."

Lovey was focusing on Royal's lips as she spoke and feeling it in the deepest part of herself. If they kept talking in this way Lovey might completely swoon and have to be carried back to the house. She looked out over the pond to give her heart a moment to slow its pace. Feeling a bit more in control of her desire, she turned back to Royal.

"You should submit your work for publication, Royal. From the small samples I've read, you're quite good."

"Yeah, maybe someday. I wouldn't even know where to start with that."

Lovey sank into Royal so that she could kiss her cheek. She was enjoying the comfort of Royal's arms around her, but she needed to put a little space between them or she'd be so distracted she wouldn't be able to focus on their conversation. She turned completely, pulling her skirt around her knees, and leaned back on her arm.

"I only have another couple of months before I start teaching." Lovey changed the subject and pulled at another clover. She was searching for some luck.

"I didn't know you had an assignment."

"My father arranged it. That's why I came back here. It wasn't working for me to stay in Chicago by myself, and I guess there's more of a need for teachers in rural areas."

"Yeah, because the pay isn't great and teachers have to be careful not to teach radical notions, like the Earth is round."

"You can't be serious." Lovey leaned back and studied Royal's face.

"There was this really cute teacher a few years ago who was asked to leave because she taught her students that the Earth was round."

"I'll ignore the fact that you said she was cute for a moment. Don't people in Georgia know the Earth is round?"

"Some do. And you'll be happy to know I'm one of them, but others follow scripture to the letter. Several local deacons brought in the Bible and showed her the verse about 'the four corners of the Earth.' If the Earth were round there'd be no corners and that would be in conflict with the Good Book."

"In that case, this might be a very short career path I'm on."

They both laughed.

"I should probably get to some chores or Momma will be after me. Can I offer you a ride home?" Royal stood and extended a hand to Lovey.

"That would be sweet, thank you." They began walking back toward the way they'd come. Lovey twirled a four-leaf clover between her fingers as they sauntered through the tall grassy field.

When they reached the pole shed where the truck and tractor were parked, Ned was just putting some old weathered boards into the back of the truck. As they drew closer, he gave them a wave and a smile.

"Well, if it isn't the bee charmer herself."

"I'll thank you to keep a lady's secrets, kind sir. It's Ned, right?"

Ned bowed deeply. "At your service."

"Come on, I'll give you a ride home before Ned here tries to steal you away from me."

CHAPTER TWENTY

Who was that?"

Lovey had just stepped through the door and quickly realized that her father had seen Royal drop her off at the end of the gravel driveway. He had pulled his spectacles off and was peering out through a small opening in the drapes to get a better view of the driver. Lovey knew that a vague answer wouldn't satisfy her father this time, so she decided to answer truthfully and try to seem as nonchalant about it as possible so as not to raise his curiosity further.

"I was out for a walk and Royal Duval offered me a ride home."

"Royal Duval, you say?"

"Yes. Interesting name, don't you think?" Lovey flopped into a chair and began to flip through a hardcover book she'd lifted from the small side table nearby. She casually noted the title, *The Epistle to the Romans*, by Karl Barth. *Riveting.* But she decided the book might provide a distraction from the discussion of Royal. "Is this an interesting book?"

"It is. It's a rethinking of our theological heritage from Paul."

"Which is?" Lovey knew the book of Romans probably as well as her father; she'd read it many times. But she also knew that explaining things to her made him feel needed.

"Barth posits that God is revealed in the cross." He pulled his glasses off as he dropped into the overstuffed chair across from her. "He rebuffs previous attempts to align God with aspects of human culture."

Lovey paused on a few pages as she continued to flip through the book. She wasn't a fan of the apostle Paul, an opinion she kept largely to herself. Hers would not be a welcomed opinion to any Southern Baptist congregation. Where Christ was inclusive and expansive, Paul seemed small to her. And then there was his not so generous view of women. No, Lovey was not a fan of Paul. He was the apostle who came long after Christ's death. He'd been a Roman, part of the ruling class that persecuted the very sect he now evangelized. Caravaggio's famous painting of Paul's conversion on the road to Damascus was one of her favorites from her art history studies for the emotion of the intimate event it captured, but still she remained suspicious.

"You know I'm not a fan of Paul." Lovey closed the book and put it back on top of the other books stacked neatly on the small table beside her chair. She gave her father her most sincere look. "I don't really need to rethink him."

"Lovey, you know how it bothers me to hear you say this. We've been over this before and—"

"Then why don't we just agree to disagree and I'll go start dinner." She smiled at him, hoping that her tone sounded more playful than argumentative.

Her father let out a long sigh. "I'll let the topic rest for the moment."

She smiled as she left the room. Royal's name had not come up again. Her distraction had been a success, for the time being.

Royal stirred the bubbling hot vat of mash with a long wooden stick. The works of the still were shaded from view by a dense canopy of hardwoods. Royal nodded at Ned, indicating for him to spell her. He took the stick and began his turn at the pot. They'd headed up to the still after Royal had driven Lovey home and finished other farm chores. The sun was dipping low in the sky as Royal reclined on a nearby stump to watch Ned work. She pulled a long piece of dry grass and put the end of it in her mouth absently.

"So, things seem to be going well with you and the bee

charmer." Ned wiped at the sweat on his forehead from the heat coming off the cooking pot.

"So far."

"Don't try to be all nonchalant about it. I can tell you really like her by the way you act around her."

"What's that supposed to mean?" Royal leaned forward on the stump to get a better view of Ned's expression.

"I've never seen you act nervous around a girl before."

"I'm not nervous around her."

"Says you."

They were quiet for a minute or two before Royal spoke again. "Do you think a girl like Lovey could really go for someone like me?" Royal wasn't so sure. She felt somehow like under more thorough examination on Lovey's part she wouldn't measure up.

"She seems like she likes you. What's not to like about the Duvals, right?"

But before she could respond to Ned, they heard rustling footsteps coming toward them. Royal stood up just as Wade appeared at the edge of the small clearing around the distilling rig.

Wade didn't speak but instead, after hesitating for only an instant, went right for Royal. He grabbed her by the shirtfront and shoved her to the ground.

"What the hell?" Royal scrambled backward and got to her feet.

"I should be askin' you that question." He came at her again, and she shifted so that a thick tree trunk blocked his reach.

"What's the matter?" Ned asked.

"You stay outta this!" Ned visibly flinched when Wade jabbed an accusing finger through the air in his direction.

"Royal, your momma let it slip that you was with Lovey Porter today. That she actually came by the damn house!"

"So?"

"So her father is Abraham Edwards. He and Boyd Cotton are thick as thieves, that's the *so*!" She tried to move away from him again but stumbled. Wade grabbed her arm and slapped her hard across the face.

Royal had suffered Wade's verbal assaults before, but he'd never hit her. The sting of it tingled across her face. He slapped her again, and she fell backward from the blow. Ned was edging toward them now. Royal motioned him away because she knew he'd had more than his share of his father's temper.

"Don't hit me again, damn you." She touched her face, and when she pulled her fingers away there was blood. She wasn't sure if it was from her lip or her nose because the whole side of her face registered the pain of the blow.

"Well, then you better fucking stay away from Edwards's daughter. I tolerate your queerie ways, but when you bring that business right to our doorstep you've gone too far." Wade stood over her with clenched fists. She didn't get up for fear he'd swing at her again.

"You're not my father, Wade. Quit acting like you have any say over my life."

"No, I'm not your father. Thank God for that small favor."

"You don't get to tell me who I spend time with."

"I do and I will." He reached for her, pulling her up by the front of her soiled shirt.

When he pulled back to strike, Ned grabbed his arm, which seemed to enrage him further. He spun on Ned and landed a punch to his jaw that sent him to the ground hard. But Ned's distraction gave Royal just enough time to get to her feet. She put the mash pot between them, the steam from the bubbling mixture creating an eerie, distorted image of Wade's face from Royal's viewpoint.

Fury surged through her system. She was looking around for something she could use to even the fight when Ned grabbed her and pushed her back toward the tree line.

He urgently whispered in her ear as she pushed against him trying to break away from his grasp. "Let it go. He ain't worth it. You can't win this."

"You better fucking leave and don't let me catch you showing that bitch around the place again."

Ned kept pushing her back away from the still and down the winding path through the woods back toward the farm. She pulled away from him at one point with every intention to head back and confront Wade.

"Don't! Don't let him get to you! You'll just get yourself hurt." He stepped into her path to block her. "Trust me on this. I know what I'm talking about."

"God, how do you put up with him? He's getting worse." Royal was pacing in a small circle. She ran her hand through her hair trying to calm down. "If he says or does one thing to Lovey...one thing..."

"He won't. He wouldn't."

"The day he takes over from Granddad is my last day. It should be yours too."

"Just walk it off, Royal. Walk it off."

Royal nodded and reluctantly strode ahead of Ned back down the wooded path toward her mother's house. Her face stung and ached from the strike of Wade's palm, but her heart rate was finally starting to slow to a normal pace.

Chapter Twenty-one

The much-anticipated Friday night dinner hour finally arrived. Royal pulled in the driveway and grabbed the flowers she'd picked that lay in a clump on the seat beside her. They were wildflowers of blue and yellow with a few groupings of Queen Anne's lace thrown in. She practically skipped up the porch steps but paused before knocking, her hand suspended an inch from the door. What if Lovey's father was still in the house? She looked around for somewhere to stash the flowers, which now seemed like an impulsive mistake, when Lovey opened the door. A big smile spread across her face when she saw the flowers in Royal's hand.

"Oh, these are for you." Royal handed her the flowers. "I had a momentary panic that your father might still be here and so, well, these might have seemed awkward if that had been the case."

"He's long gone. And I love flowers, thank you." Lovey stepped aside so that Royal could cross the threshold.

This really felt like a date. Royal rubbed her hands against her trouser-clad thighs. Were her palms actually sweating? *Pull it together!* She realized Lovey was watching her and so she smiled.

"Come in the kitchen. Dinner is just about ready and I'll put these in some water." Royal followed her. She couldn't help noticing Lovey's hips as she walked. The summer weight cotton dress was tailored perfectly to hang low at her waist to highlight her slender, girlish curves. Lovey was so pretty it took Royal's breath away.

Lovey looked over her shoulder at Royal as she trimmed the flowers and put them in a tall glass vase. The look she gave Royal hit her full in the chest. She nervously cleared her throat for fear that Lovey was at that instant reading her thoughts, all of which had moved ahead to what she hoped would be happening much later in the evening.

"What are you thinking?" Lovey asked. Having finished with the flowers, she set them at the end of the kitchen table.

"Nothing and everything."

"You really are a poet, aren't you?" Lovey motioned toward a place setting already on the table. "Why don't you sit down and relax?"

"I'll sit down, but I'm not sure I can relax. Am I the only one who's nervous? Why am I so nervous?" She asked the question aloud, but directed it more to herself.

"I'm not sure, but I'm a little nervous myself. I'm glad I'm not the only one." Lovey poured iced tea for both of them and set a glass in front of Royal. "Why don't we just sit and talk until it passes?"

"Okay." Royal let out a sigh and leaned back in her chair. "Can I help with anything?"

Lovey looked up and checked the kitchen clock. "No, everything is ready, I think. I made baked chicken with potatoes and carrots. Nothing fancy. I hope that's okay."

"Anything will be great." Royal's stomach was so full of butterflies she expected not to be able to eat much anyway.

Lovey busied herself serving the food. She leaned over Royal's shoulder, balancing one hand there as she settled the plate in front of her. She kissed Royal lightly on the cheek before taking her own seat. She watched with pleasure as Royal took a few bites of the dinner she'd prepared and smiled in her direction.

Not for the first time, Lovey was struck by how truly classically handsome Royal was. Not quite feminine, not quite masculine, but rather androgynously good-looking. She sensed she was making Royal a little self-conscious by studying her so intently. Averting her eyes with great effort, she tasted a few forkfuls of her supper.

"Ever since I saw the bullet hole in your car I've been wanting to ask more about what you do." Lovey took another bite, chewing slowly, watching Royal's face again.

"What do you want to know?"

"I guess I want to know why you do it? Why deliver moonshine at such risk?"

"Well, it's not the risk I'm after. Oh, well, maybe a little risk is invigorating if I were to be truthful. But what it really is for me is the driving. I love to drive fast."

"You could drive fast without the moonshine."

"I suppose you're right, but I wouldn't get paid to do it."

"So it's the driving and the money then?"

Royal seemed to be considering the question. "Yes. If I could figure out another way to get paid for driving I'd surely consider it."

"Do you ever drink the stuff you deliver?"

"No, I really prefer whiskey."

"I guess I don't know the difference." Lovey realized her Southern Baptist upbringing had her at a disadvantage when it came to spirits of the liquid denomination.

"Whiskey is aged in oak. Some folks say moonshine is whiskey without the wood. Moonshine is young and raw."

The low tenor in Royal's voice as she described the difference gave Lovey's stomach a twist. *Young and raw, indeed.*

"What were we sipping the other night at your place?" asked Lovey.

"That was whiskey."

"Oh. I rather liked the way the warmth of it spread down my throat."

Lovey realized as they talked that she couldn't entirely relax in her father's house. It was as if he'd left his ghostly presence to actively disapprove of her behavior. As if the walls themselves would not keep her secrets. She wanted to leave and go to Royal's place as soon as possible.

They finished the food and Lovey refilled their tea. The evening sun was low, so the room had taken on a warm afternoon glow as the sky reddened near the horizon.

"Oh, I almost forgot. I have something for you." Lovey stood and left the room, her short heels clicking against the hardwood floor as she walked the distance to her bedroom and back. She handed a small brown package to Royal.

"For me?" Royal looked at her with a questioning expression.

"I asked my father to pick it up at the bookstore in Gainesville."

"Your father picked up a gift for me?" Royal's voice rose with surprise.

"Well, he thought it was for me. But all along it was for you. Open it."

Royal turned the small slender package over in her hand before she tore at the brown paper and string to find what was inside. A book. A poetry book. The title on the cover read *Bright Ambush* by Audrey Wurdemann. She looked up at Lovey. "You bought me poetry." Royal opened to the first poem and read one line aloud.

"The author was the first woman to win the Pulitzer for Poetry. And she was only twenty-four years old."

"The same age as me." Royal was taken aback by such a thoughtful gift. She leaned over and pulled Lovey into a kiss. "Thank you. I love it."

"I hope you enjoy it once you've read it and that it brings you inspiration."

"*Bright Ambush*. Great title."

Lovey started clearing plates while Royal thumbed through the thin volume of poetry. "Should we go soon?"

"Yes. Absolutely." Royal didn't want to say it out loud, but she felt just the least bit unsettled being in the reverend's house, thinking what she'd been thinking earlier about Lovey. That unease on top of her butterfly-filled stomach made her fidget, and she was sure Lovey could tell that she couldn't fully relax.

She stood near Lovey with a towel as they washed the dinner dishes and tidied up. Royal wondered what it would be like to have this treat daily. Sharing evening meals and then the chores that followed before snuggling up together for sleep, or not sleeping, the sacred rituals of the day-to-day. It was a dream that Royal hoped someday could be her reality. But she didn't want to get ahead of herself.

❖

It was dark and just past nine o'clock when they drove toward Royal's rented room near the center of town. They were almost there when something off to the side caught Royal's eye. Lovey noticed Royal crane her neck looking toward the dark space near the alley between the old Mill building and Talbot's Feed Store. Royal eased off the road, cut the engine, and stepped out of the car. Lovey tried to read Royal's body language, which seemed suddenly tense.

"What is it?" Lovey leaned over from the passenger side trying to peer out the driver's side door.

"You should stay in the car." Royal reached into a small space behind the front seat and removed a leather holster and revolver.

"Royal, what's going on?" Lovey was afraid.

"Everything is going to be okay. And just so you know, I don't like guns." Royal removed the revolver and released the cylinder, spinning it to check that it was loaded. "But ever since the other night I've felt better having one nearby."

Sounds of a woman's voice caught Lovey's attention as Royal walked away from the car. She could see that there were at least three, no, four figures in the low glow cast from the overhead oil lamp at the corner of the Mill.

Not someone who enjoyed being told what to do, she ignored Royal's request to stay put. Lovey scooted across the front seat and slid out the door for a closer look. She could make out the shapes of three men and one woman. The lighting wasn't great, but she could see enough to know the men were white and the young woman, who seemed to be in some distress, was black.

Lovey heard Royal call to the men as she approached. "I think you fellas should move along." Her voice sounded strong, confident.

Royal had asked her to stay in the car, but curiosity and fear for Royal got the better of her, so Lovey stepped nearer still. She was far enough to be able to make a quick retreat to the parked sedan but close enough to hear the exchange.

One of the men turned at the sound of Royal's voice. He was

rough looking. His face covered with a few days' growth of beard and his clothes dusty. "This is none of your concern. Leave it be."

"I'm making it my concern." Royal kept the gun down at her side, blocked from their view. "Grace, do you need a ride home?"

"Yeah—" The woman started to speak, but one of the men stopped her, placing his hand in the center of her chest and shoving her back against the uneven brick wall of the building. A few more steps and they would have been far enough into the dark alley that Royal wouldn't have seen them. Lovey suspected that they'd driven by at just the right moment to intervene.

"You know this darkie?" The man spoke again and turned to face Royal while the two other men held Grace against the building. Grace looked to be in her twenties, with a slim, girlish build. Even in the dim light, Lovey could see that one of them was moving his hands up the top of the woman's blue gingham dress in a far too intimate way.

"You best tell your friend there to take his hand off her before I relieve him of his ability to use it." Royal had raised the revolver and pointed it at the man who was fondling Grace.

"That's tall talk for a girl. You think just because you dress like a man that makes you one?" He took a step toward Royal but stopped when he heard the unmistakable click as she cocked the hammer.

"I don't need to be a man to know how a woman should be treated."

There was a small scuffle as one of the men reached for the hem of Grace's dress, and she dropped the small brown bag she'd been carrying to the dirt, needing both hands to fend off his roaming advances. A small whimper escaped Grace's lips before one of the two men nearest Grace covered her mouth and began shoving her toward the shadows, boldly ignoring Royal's request.

"Let her go. Now." Royal took a step toward the group, the pistol held high in front of her.

Lovey was several feet away from the scene that was unfolding, but panic began to settle in her chest. Her heart pounded like she'd just run a foot race, and she was certain her hands were shaking. Royal seemed rock solid. The only evidence that she was at all under duress was the muscle in her jaw that clenched and released each time Grace was touched. Obviously, from the subtle emotion playing across her face, Royal knew this woman and cared about her.

"I said, let her go. And that's the last time I'm gonna say it before I start shooting kneecaps."

One of the men closest to Grace looked toward Royal for a moment. His eyes looked bleary; his motions indicated he was probably under the influence of alcohol. He was thinner than the man who'd first confronted Royal, but just as worn out and scruffy looking. His overalls were patched at various spots.

"What are you, some kinda nigger lover?" His speech was slightly slurred, but there was no mistaking the words he'd meant as an insult.

Royal's jaw clenched again, but then she spoke. "If by that you mean do I care about someone who's earned my respect, regardless of skin color, then yes, I suppose I am."

The larger man in front, the one who'd spoken first, made a move toward Royal, and without changing her stance, she lowered the revolver and fired a warning shot between his feet. The look of shock on his face showed that he'd doubted she would pull the trigger, until now. The sound of the discharged round pierced the night air, cutting through the muffled music that had been drifting through the alleyway from the piano inside the Mill. It echoed loudly across the wood-sided feed store.

The music stopped, and before the three men could respond, two figures came around the corner from where the entrance to the drinking joint was. One of them, Lovey recognized from the feed store, Frank Mosby. He stepped out of the shadow of the building and looked in Royal's direction. Frank was a huge man, probably in his mid thirties. Backlit as he was from the filtered streetlamp behind him, he looked like Goliath. The second man who moved to stand at his shoulder was smaller, and she didn't recognize him, but his body language seemed to indicate that he would follow Frank's lead. A few other revelers now appeared near the corner to investigate the ruckus.

"Royal, is there a problem?" Frank moved next to her, but faced the three men who still surrounded Grace.

"You'll have to ask this fellow. I was just asking them nicely to leave, but they seem reluctant."

With two large strides, Frank was close enough to the man in front to grab him by his shirt and pull him up on his toes. "Is there a reason you're still here?"

The man shoved at Frank to no avail. After a moment, Frank released him with a backward shove. He fell into the dirt before scrambling to his feet, visibly angry but backing away as he dusted himself off.

"Come on. Let's get out of here. Nothing is worth this much trouble." His two companions reluctantly released Grace, who slumped against the side of the building, the wet paths of tears on her dark cheeks reflecting the light from the streetlamp.

Royal lowered the pistol, but she and Frank stood where they were until the three strangers had climbed into their ancient battered truck and only a trailing dust cloud was left as a reminder of their passage into the darkening night. Lovey crossed the space between them, standing on Royal's other side and looking down the dirt road where the vehicle had just disappeared.

"Did you know them?" Royal asked Frank.

"No, I didn't recognize them. Just passing through I suppose. They must have been inside drinking, but I didn't take note of them." Frank turned to look at Royal. "You should have come in and gotten help. Especially since Miss Porter was with you."

"Well, I asked Miss Porter to stay in the car." Royal gave Lovey a sideways glance, and Lovey responded with a sheepish smile. "I didn't think they'd be dumb enough to come at me with me having the Colt." Royal eased the hammer forward on the pistol. "Guess I was wrong."

"You're okay then?" Frank looked from Royal over to where

Grace was gathering up the contents of the brown paper bag that had spilled, although he didn't acknowledge her by name.

"We're fine. Go back to your fun. And thanks."

Frank nodded and smiled, slapping Royal on the back with his large hand as he passed by. "Okay, fellas, show's over. And I need another drink!" Laughing voices responded as the group that had gathered shuffled noisily back into the Mill. After a moment, the music started up again.

Now that they were alone in the street, Royal went to Grace. Lovey followed a few steps behind. Grace was wiping at her cheeks with the back of her hand and sniffing.

"Here, let me take the bag for you." Lovey reached out, offering the only assistance she could think of. Grace handed over the parcel and leaned into Royal.

"Come on, Grace. We'll drive you home. Everything's okay now." Still holding the revolver in one hand, Royal put her other arm around Grace's shoulders and ushered her toward the car. She opened the door, pulling the bucket seat forward to allow Grace to climb in the back.

CHAPTER TWENTY-TWO

They were silent for a few moments as Royal turned the car and headed south out of town, toward where Lovey assumed Grace lived. Royal pulled a handkerchief out of her pocket and handed it over her shoulder to Grace.

"Don't say anything about this to Mama, okay?" Grace dabbed at her eyes with the crisp white linen. "She would just worry."

Royal glanced at Grace's reflected image in the rearview mirror. "I won't."

Lovey could see Royal's knuckles whiten as she clenched the steering wheel. She glanced at the mirror again as she spoke to Grace. "Did they hurt you? Are you hurt?"

"No," came the muffled reply.

"You shouldn't have been walking by yourself at this hour." Royal's tone was even, but Lovey heard an edge to it.

"Sam was supposed to give me a ride, but he had to leave early today. His grandmother was ill. One of the boys came to get him so that he could fetch a doctor." Grace reached and placed her hand on Royal's shoulder. "Please don't say anything to Sam either. There's nothing he can do about it now and he'd just be mad."

"Well, that would make two of us then." Royal stared at the road. "I'm not angry with you. You know that, right? It's not that you did anything wrong, Grace. It's just that the world isn't a safe place. Sometimes even here, where it should be."

There was silence for a few moments before Lovey turned

sideways in the front seat so that she could look at Grace. "I'm Lovey Porter." She extended her hand.

"Grace Watkins." Grace accepted Lovey's hand, meeting her gaze directly.

"Sorry. I should have introduced you two." Royal smiled for the first time since they'd climbed back in the car.

They drove the rest of the way in silence, finally turning onto a narrow, rutted path that could barely be called a road. The deepest darkness surrounded the small glowing circles cast in front of them by the headlights. A small house began to take shape in the distance. A warm glow coming from small squares at the front of the narrow, unpainted house hinted at its existence in the dark grove that surrounded it. Royal pulled up close to the raised porch at the front of the house. A hound dog barked and made a halfhearted attempt to get up, but when someone yelled from inside, the dog quickly resumed its prone position.

Lovey climbed out first, pulling the seat forward to allow Grace to exit. What Lovey could see of the yard in the dark was mostly dirt, a pile of wood stacked haphazardly near the end of the porch, an axe sunk into a stump, and various small wooden boxes filled with what looked like bottles. She turned just in time to see Royal pull Grace into a hug. Grace threw her arms around Royal's neck and whispered something in her ear that Lovey couldn't make out. She felt a twinge of jealousy that Grace had so easily embraced Royal. They clearly knew each other well. This was one more part of Royal's personal history that Lovey had yet to uncover. The hug ended just as an older woman stepped onto the porch.

"Royal, is that you?" the matronly woman yelled from the top step.

"Yes, ma'am." Royal smiled and moved into the lights from the car near the bottom porch step. She had retrieved the parcel from the car and handed the bag to Grace. "I was just giving Grace a ride home."

"Well, then come in here. I just took a fruit pie out of the oven. It needs to get ate while it's hot."

"You know I love your pie more than air itself, but I have a friend with me and I should probably get going."

The woman that Lovey assumed was Grace's mother leaned down to see who was in the car, but the glare of the headlights no doubt made it impossible to get a clear view.

"Y'all both come in. There's plenty. Now I won't take no for an answer." Grace walked past the woman and into the house. Royal stepped back and leaned into the window of the car.

"What do you say? Do you want to stay for a minute and have some dessert?" Royal's handsome face seemed to have lost the weight of tension it carried just twenty minutes earlier, as she smiled through the open window at Lovey.

"It's hard to say no to dessert."

"Come on then." Royal opened the door and extended her hand for Lovey to slide over and take. When their fingers touched, Lovey felt it all the way to her toes. A surge of warmth. Her world had been expanding since the first night she'd met Royal, hanging upside down in her overturned car. It seemed tonight was to be no different.

As they stepped on the porch, the older woman wiped her hands on a white apron before greeting them with genuine friendliness. "I'm Ella Watkins, Grace's mother. Any friend of Royal's is surely welcome at my table any time."

"Hi, Mrs. Watkins, I'm Lovey Porter. Thank you for your hospitality."

Ella, who Lovey's father might have described as pleasingly plump, put an arm around each of them and ushered them inside. The cozy, lantern-lit kitchen smelled of a wood stove and baked goods. Lovey quickly noted the worn and threadbare furniture and fixtures in the main living space, which opened into an eat-in kitchen. But whatever the house may have been lacking in décor, the rich, sweet aroma of baked dessert more than made up for.

Grace smiled at them both as they each took a seat at the large square table in the center of the room. In the lantern light Lovey could now see more details of Grace's features. She was pretty, with caramel-colored skin and high cheekbones, her hair neatly pulled back into a curled knot at her neck. Two plates, heaped with what looked like blackberry pie, were settled in front of them along with a cup of coffee for each.

"Cream?" Grace motioned toward Lovey's cup with a glass jug of frothy milk.

"No, thanks. Black is good." As soon as she'd said the words, Lovey was struck by what she'd said. Royal quickly came to her rescue.

"Yes, it is." Royal took a huge bite of pie and everyone laughed. Lovey felt herself relax too. She took a smaller bite than Royal's, but her senses immediately reacted to the flavor explosion of the sweet fruit pie filling the moment it hit her tongue.

"This pie is amazing." Lovey looked in Mrs. Watkins's direction with genuine admiration.

"My momma has the magic touch for baking." Grace smiled and sipped her coffee as she held it lightly in both hands with her elbows resting on the table. The shadow of what had happened earlier was still visible in the sadness at the edges of her eyes, but she thought Grace hid it well. She seemed to study Lovey across the rim of her coffee cup, and Lovey wondered what Grace thought of her. She wondered what Grace thought she'd been doing out with Royal. From the way Grace studied her, Lovey assumed she knew exactly what was going on between them. The realization that her attraction to Royal had been uncovered made Lovey's cheeks flame hotly.

"Hush now, Grace. Y'all know if you just add enough sugar to anything you can turn it into pie filling. Even the sourest grape desires to be sweetened." Ella patted her daughter's arm good-naturedly. "Now, Lovey, tell us about yourself. Who are your people? You said your last name was Porter? I don't recognize that name."

"Porter is my married name." Lovey watched Grace's eyes widen slightly as she reacted to this revelation.

"You're married then? And your husband lets you run around with Royal?"

"Hey, I'm sittin' right here." Royal took another bite of pie as Ella gave her a wink.

"He, um, he passed away. A year ago." The mood at the table suddenly shifted, and Ella reached over to place a comforting hand on Lovey's.

"Oh, darlin', I'm awful sorry. You're so young. Was he as young as you?"

"He was only a year older."

"Such a shame."

"And no children?"

"No, ma'am."

"Lovey moved back to live with her father, Rev. Edwards, you know, he's pastor at the Baptist church." Royal spared Lovey from having to say more by offering a bit more detail on her behalf.

"Well, we're glad you're with us, although we're sorry for the circumstances." Ella warmed up everyone's coffee with a battered tin pot from the stove. "This is a good place to live. Good people. You'll be happy here, Lovey."

"I think you might be right, Mrs. Watkins."

"Please, you eat at my table, you gotta call me Ella."

Something caught Lovey's eye. She leaned forward just enough to see a T-shirt clad youngster leaning shyly against the door frame from a side room off the kitchen. Lovey smiled at the child, and he obviously took that as an invitation. He slid up next to Royal, leaning against her chair.

"What's this?" Royal reached around and playfully pulled the young boy into her lap. "Who's tryin' to sneak up on me?" The child giggled as Royal tickled his ribs lightly and he wiggled in her lap.

"Tyler Watkins, you are supposed to be in bed, young man." Ella tried to give the boy a stern expression, but Lovey suspected from the motherly tone of her voice that it was easier for her to nurture than to discipline. The boy clearly wasn't afraid of her, but leaned into Royal for protection nonetheless.

"Okay, Tyler, one taste and then back to bed." Royal handed

him her fork and watched him shovel two quick bites before he scurried back to bed.

❖

After another half hour at the Watkins place, they drove down the rutted path back to the graded county road. Royal hesitated before easing the car back on the roadway.

"Are you tired?" Royal leaned forward on the steering wheel and looked in Lovey's direction.

"Not particularly." The truth was, between the coffee and the encounter with meanness earlier, Lovey was rather wound up.

Royal rewarded her with a smile, and instead of turning toward town, they headed in the opposite direction.

"I thought you might like to see something before we drive back to town." Royal volunteered before Lovey could ask the question about where they were going. She couldn't imagine how they could squeeze much more into this night, but she was willing to give it a try. It was just past ten o'clock, and she knew her father wouldn't be home from the revival until late the next morning.

Once the altar calls started, sometimes the event would then continue on into the wee hours. He'd be exhausted and emotionally spent when he finally returned home. He'd always told Lovey that the best time to do the Lord's work was in the Devil's hours, which she assumed, based on the hours the annual revival kept, was between ten at night and four in the morning.

Lovey regarded Royal's strong profile from the passenger seat. She was fighting a strong desire to slide over so that she could place her hand on Royal's thigh, but the raised stick shift seemed like a barrier, not to mention the fact that she was unsure of how Royal was feeling at the moment. They'd just gone through a tense standoff, and someone who was clearly close to Royal had been threatened. Maybe Royal would not welcome an advance from Lovey at the moment, despite the fact that the air between them seemed thick with desire. Did Royal feel it too? The moonlight highlighting Royal's features made Lovey's heart flutter like a hummingbird. She felt light-headed and had to force herself to turn and look out the window at the dark woods roving past the moving car.

After only a few more moments, they turned off the main road onto a narrow, rutted road that descended in gradual switchbacks until the trees around them opened up to reveal a small, smooth-surfaced lake.

Lovey leaned forward in her seat as the car slowed not too far from the edge of the lake. The moon was incredibly bright, and with the surface of the dark water so glassy, the glowing orb was reflected back at itself, doubling its enchanting luminosity.

"Oh, Royal. This is magical."

"Come on. It's even a better view from outside the car."

Royal had pulled alongside the lake so that once they were out of the car she leaned back on its black lacquer surface, resting one boot on the footboard and sinking her hands in her pockets. Lovey walked down to the water's edge and lingered for a moment, looking at the reflected celestial sphere before returning to stand near the car. The summer air, despite the late hour, was pleasantly warm.

"How do you know Grace?" Lovey had sublimated her curiosity as long as possible. She needed to know more about the woman they'd just rescued and how that woman was connected to Royal.

"Grace's grandmother basically raised my father after my grandma passed. And after Grace's grandmother passed and my dad was grown, her mother just kept taking care of my granddad." Royal switched her stance, shifting so that her other foot now was on the footboard. "Ella always seemed to make an extra pie by accident, or extra cornbread or somethin' that she'd bring by the house."

"That's very kind."

"I guess over the years the Watkins women just sort of became like family. Grace and I spent a lot of time together as kids." Royal put both feet on the ground and scuffed at the dirt with the toe of her boot. "I didn't know until I was older that Grace and I were different and that others expected our friendship to have limits. And even now that I know, I don't understand it. I never will."

"My father always preaches that the Bible is against the mixing of the races." Lovey uttered the statement without conviction, crossing her arms in front of her chest as if the words embarrassed her.

"And do you believe that?" Royal cocked her head in Lovey's direction.

"I was raised not to question the Bible, but—"

"But?"

"But sometimes the words in scripture don't echo the truth I feel in my heart. I don't believe God would create any creature of lesser worth. It sometimes feels like we bend the words to support our own biases. Don't get me started on all the things the Bible says about women that I don't agree with."

"It's a book, based on ancient scrolls, translated by imperfect men. I think it's good to question its content."

Lovey smiled. "I'll invite you to Sunday lunch the next time I'm debating scripture with my father."

Lovey leaned into Royal, putting her head on her shoulder. "I must admit, this evening has taken turns I didn't expect. I suppose when I spend time with you I should be prepared for anything from a rescue mission to a theological debate."

Royal kissed the top of her head. "Maybe we should see if we can get back to our original plan. Do you still want to come over to my place?"

"Most definitely." Lovey squeezed Royal tightly before releasing her so that they could climb back in the car. Anticipation settled into every nerve ending as she slid into the seat next to Royal.

Chapter Twenty-three

They faced each other as Royal traced the outline of Lovey's face with her fingertips. Royal, wearing her undershirt and trousers, stood facing Lovey, who was wearing only her slip. Royal thought Lovey was the sexiest woman she'd ever seen. She slid her palms down Lovey's ribs, then moved her hands back up a little so that her thumbs brushed across Lovey's nipples, bringing them to sharp points under the satin fabric.

Lovey closed her eyes and leaned into Royal. With eyes closed, she unfastened Royal's belt and trousers so that they slumped in a pile around her feet. Royal kicked them off to the side and pushed Lovey toward the edge of the bed.

After falling onto the bed, Royal allowed her hand to drift down to the hem of the slip, which she slowly pushed up and over Lovey's head. She paused with Lovey's arms constrained over her head in the silky tangle. With Lovey's arms confined above her head, Royal pushed up the bra to expose the tender mound of Lovey's breast and took it into her mouth. Royal felt Lovey shudder beneath her. Royal released Lovey's arms so that she could focus on Lovey's milky smooth skin, and as she did, Lovey managed to reach behind and unhook her bra, pulling it free and giving Royal full access.

Royal pulled away from her for a moment and sat back on her heels. She was between Lovey's bent knees when she slowly and seductively slipped Lovey's underwear off. For a moment, she sat looking down at Lovey, fully exposed to her. Royal slowly moved her fingertips down the inside of Lovey's thighs and then back up to her knees, all the while never losing eye contact.

Lovey allowed Royal to take her in. She'd never exposed herself in such a way to anyone, but rather than embarrassment, all she felt from Royal was adoration.

After removing her remaining clothes, Royal slowly moved her full weight on top of Lovey, settling her narrow hips between Lovey's thighs. Royal traced the outside curve of Lovey's hip before bringing her hand up to cup Lovey's cheek. She spoke only one word, softly, against Lovey's lips. "Beautiful."

Royal traced a finger down the center of Lovey's chest, over her stomach before teasing the spot between her legs. Royal began to kiss Lovey deeply, at the same time she pushed slowly inside.

Lovey moaned against Royal's mouth and breathlessly uttered the only word that came to mind when she was alone with Royal. "More." *More, more, more.*

Royal obliged, urgently pressing fully inside as Lovey pulsed and moved beneath her. Lovey offered herself completely and without reservation to Royal's infinite exploration.

Royal continued to rhythmically push in and out until Lovey climaxed under her. She clung to her and tightened her thighs around Royal's hips.

Royal had never been sexually intimate with a woman she knew she was falling in love with. She'd been infatuated with women and physically attracted to women she'd slept with, but this was different. Royal felt unmasked, raw, like a nerve ending exposed to open air. She became acutely aware that in this moment Lovey could crush her with a single word.

As if sensing her thoughts, Lovey pulled Royal down into a kiss, running her fingers through the hair at the back of Royal's neck and skimming the nails of her other hand down Royal's back. "I want you so badly," she whispered, close to Royal's ear, sending chills up and down Royal's arm.

Royal slid up slightly on top of Lovey so that her breasts hovered just above Lovey's slightly swollen lips. Lovey took the hint, and as Royal grasped the iron railing of the headboard with both hands, Lovey took first one and then the other of Royal's nipples into her mouth. As she worked with her tongue and teased with her teeth on Royal's chest, Royal began to move her center against Lovey's thigh.

The wetness Lovey felt slide across her leg brought forth her own arousal again. Royal was going to bring them both to climax just by moving, now roughly on top of her, pressing against her, moaning softly as the orgasm claimed her.

Royal collapsed on top of Lovey and then rolled over onto her back. Lovey stroked Royal's chest with her fingers and then trailed them down so that she could tease the spot between Royal's legs that was still wet and swollen. Lovey didn't really know what she was doing except following her instincts. She wanted to be inside Royal. She wanted to claim that place that she now felt was hers. Lovey shifted her body on top of Royal's, keeping her hand between them as she continued to slowly stroke.

Royal moaned and pulled Lovey into a kiss. "God, Lovey, what you do to me." She was breathing hard and the words came out in a rushed whisper against Lovey's mouth as she climaxed.

❖

The room was dark except for the moonlight sifting through a broadleaf hardwood near the window. Lovey thought Royal was asleep. Her breathing seemed deep and even. Lovey smoothed the ever-unruly clump of blond hair off Royal's forehead and tenderly caressed her cheek with her fingertips. The sheet was gathered around Royal's waist, which gave Lovey an exquisite view of her torso. She swept her open palm lightly across Royal's stomach and then up to the slight indention in the center of her chest.

In the blissful afterglow of lovemaking, a wave of sadness washed over her. What was she going to do with her feelings for Royal? What could either of them do? What could come of any of this? Reality was slowly smothering the light in her heart.

She moved on top of Royal and began to kiss her, until Royal began to stir beneath her. As Royal's eyes fluttered, Lovey pulled her hand to her mouth and sucked two of her fingers between her lips.

"Hey." Royal's voice was raspy with sleep.

"Hey," said Lovey. She was straddling Royal's waist, leaning over her.

"Couldn't sleep?"

"No, I need a little more of you." She wanted Royal's strong fingers to push inside and chase away the dark reality that was circling her before it pulled her under.

Lovey directed Royal's hand beneath her, between them. As Royal moved inside Lovey, she pressed against Royal's hand. Royal pulled Lovey's face close to hers and kissed her deeply. Even barely awake, Royal was a tender and attentive lover. Lovey buried her face in Royal's neck as the orgasm claimed her.

After the spasms subsided, she settled against Royal's shoulder and Royal pulled her close.

CHAPTER TWENTY-FOUR

Lovey was home and had food prepared for her father by the time he arrived on Saturday. As she'd anticipated, he was exhausted from his long night. When she was younger she sometimes attended these events in neighboring counties, but as she'd gotten older the allure of an all-night revival had worn off and her father no longer insisted she attend.

While he ate, she got a full accounting of the happening, scored as if it were some otherworldly sporting event: God fourteen, Satan zero.

He'd slept most of the afternoon, which left Lovey alone to enjoy flashbacks of her time with Royal. She sat in one of the upholstered chairs in the study. A Gershwin melody emanated softly from the oak casing of the radio.

Lovey leaned back and closed her eyes. There were many love songs, but none for her. She tried to imagine a different time, a different place, where the love she wanted might be possible.

Maybe it was possible and she just couldn't see clear of her own conservative upbringing. If she didn't believe in her heart that this was an unfit love, then why was she acting as if it was, expecting to have to end it? Was she so terrified of scandal that she would act against her own heart?

She was lost in her own thoughts when Joe surprised her with a visit. He'd been stopping by more and more recently for a friendly chat, or an evening stroll. This time he'd brought a two-passenger buggy and invited her for a ride. She tried to politely refuse, saying she was just about to cook dinner. Her father goaded her to accept, saying he wasn't hungry and could certainly wait for her to return.

Lovey did her best to graciously accept, but she worried that Joe was getting too attached too quickly. She did enjoy his company and she wasn't intentionally trying to lead him on, but having now spent another night with Royal, she was feeling very conflicted. If she were asked to pick between them at this moment, her heart would have swiftly and without reservation chosen Royal. But her head knew that she might be forced to make a different choice. A choice she wasn't ready to make. If pressured to do so, then Joe would not be the worst candidate. He was good-looking, polite, well mannered, and kind. He was also just the slightest bit full of himself, but in Lovey's experience, almost every man suffered under those same delusions of grandeur.

It was a gorgeous summer evening. The perfect night for a carriage ride. Joe definitely knew how to court a young woman.

"I've been thinking about us." Joe propped a foot at the side of the seat opening and let the reins droop. His horse seemed content to keep an even, slow pace without prodding.

"You have?" Lovey's stomach clenched. She didn't know what he was going to say next, and she was afraid to guess.

"Yeah, I think we're a good match, don't you?"

Okay, so he wasn't the most romantic guy. At least he was straightforward.

"I do like you, Joe. I enjoy our outings together."

"I don't want to rush you. I know that you may still need some time after losing your husband, but I was thinking…I was thinking that we might get married."

Lovey held the arm railing next to her with a white-knuckled grip. *Oh, God, I'm not ready for this.*

"I'm sorry. Did I take you by surprise?" He turned a little in the seat so he could see her face. "I know we haven't been spending time together for very long, Lovey. But, well, I'm crazy about you. You're smart, you're pretty, and I know we're probably both ready to start a family of our own."

"Joe, you're very sweet to ask. And sweet to say those things."

She put her hand on his arm for emphasis. "Can I have a little time to think about it? This is just a little bit sudden. You did catch me by surprise."

"I spoke to your father to ask permission. He will give us his blessing whenever you're ready to make it official."

Oh, no, her father already knew. He was in on this too.

"You take some time and think about it. I just wanted you to know I'm serious about you, about us. I'm not just fooling around." He hesitated a moment before he leaned over and kissed Lovey.

They'd kissed before. The sort of chaste kisses shared with someone you were not yet intimate with. Lovey had tolerated those kisses for the sake of the cover her friendship with Joe provided. But this was a different sort of kiss. Joe put his arm around her shoulders and pulled her close. He was insistent on deepening the kiss. Rather than make a scene, Lovey gave in to him. She placed a hand on his chest to keep some distance between them. They couldn't fully face each other, seated the way they were, side by side, but Joe had partially turned toward her.

As kisses go, this one wasn't terrible, but Joe certainly wasn't Royal. She longed for the soft press of Royal's lips against hers and the smell of her skin.

Joe finally released her. He smiled broadly and turned his attention back to their route. He left one arm along the seat back, just behind Lovey's shoulders. Lovey tried to appear relaxed, but inside she was a churning mess.

How far was she willing to go to cover her feelings for Royal with Joe's courtship? Joe had kissed her and she hadn't felt the slightest romantic inclination for him. She tried to access the feelings she'd once had for men, the feelings she'd had for George. She knew that these were the feelings she should naturally feel. As a woman, she should desire a man. *Should, should, should.*

She noticed that Joe was looking at her and so she tried to give him a reassuring smile. But inside, she was anything but sure of anything. *What am I going to do now?*

❖

It was late by the time Royal finished her run to North Atlanta. The drive had been easy and uneventful. If the federal boys had been out tonight they were on someone else's route because Royal never saw them. It was around two in the morning, so rather than risk waking her mother, Royal decided to stay at her place.

The room was just as she and Lovey had left it—with rumpled sheets on the bed and empty glasses on the table. She walked to the basin and splashed some water on her face to rinse away a little of the road dust. It would take a while for the adrenaline in her system to ebb enough for sleep so she decided to sit and write. She poured herself a dash of whiskey, little more than a sip, and sank into the chair in front of her typewriter.

Lines of poetry had been floating through her head all along the drive back to the hills. She wanted to write some of them down before they were lost to her.

> *Desire's flame burns across my skin*
> *I long for relief*
> *Only your lips can bring*
> *My body holds a space for you.*

Sometimes lines of poetry would present themselves to her all at once, in solid stanzas. This was one of those nights. She heard whispered phrases in her head as if she was channeling a voice from some other place or had connected with a deeper part of herself.

> *What resides in my chest is real*
> *Set against the relentless unreal*
> *Defying convention.*

Royal pushed her chair back and studied the words she'd just typed as she sipped at the whiskey. She might actually be able to sleep now that she'd gotten the words out of her head.

She moved across the room shedding her clothes as she went, leaving things where they fell until she reached the bedside in only boxers and an undershirt. Royal flopped onto the bed, careful not to slosh the whiskey from the glass. She slid down onto the pillow, keeping her head elevated just enough to sip without being hindered to swallow. The other pillow she pulled to her face smelled like Lovey. She breathed deeply. The scent of her caused a throbbing ache in Royal's chest. She wondered what Lovey was doing right at that moment. Probably sleeping. But was she craving Royal's body the way she was craving Lovey's? She hoped so.

God, she was in trouble. She'd gone and fallen for Lovey. With iridescent clarity, she knew it. She knew it as sure as she knew the sun would rise. *What am I going to do now?*

CHAPTER TWENTY-FIVE

Lovey tried to shore up her energy for a long day. First there'd be the Sunday sermon, then lunch on the lawn, and then the decoration of the graves in the old cemetery next to the narrow wood-framed white church. Relatives would return today for the homecoming celebration, so no doubt her father would take this opportunity to reach people he didn't normally see at his regular weekly service.

From her usual second row, Lovey heard the shuffling of feet as folks settled into the hard wooden pews behind her. Men's hats lined the walls, hanging from pegs. Mostly, as was the tradition, men sat on one side and women on the other. Lovey fidgeted with the drape of her dress. She just wanted to get through this day and have some time to herself.

Her father announced the theme of his message for the day, the "sins of the flesh." *You've got to be kidding.* She adjusted herself against the straight-backed seat and prepared for the worst.

"Of grave danger to Christians are the works of the flesh." Her father held his Bible aloft in front of him as he read from Galatians and then continued his admonitions. "These are the sins which wage war against our very souls. Paul has offered us a list of those sins, and I will read them to you now from the word of God."

Not Paul again! She was starting to wonder if Paul converted to Christianity just to annoy her.

Her father's voice as he recited Paul's doctrine seeped into her thoughts even as she tried to shut him out. Fornication, infidelity, adultery, premarital sex, and homosexuality, probably the absolute last topics Lovey wanted to hear about today.

Christ never mentioned any of these by name, not even during his Sermon on the Mount. Based on that observation, she'd always assumed he valued integrity and truth above all else. And nothing in her life up to this point had seemed truer or more pure than the time she was spending with Royal. How could that be a sin?

"The works of the flesh lead us down the path of moral impurity." He read a few more choice passages from Galatians before he launched into more of Paul's list of don'ts again. Today's morality lesson? She had one choice. Marry a man and have babies, end of discussion. Paul's view of relationships was extremely narrow, and apparently, so was her father's.

Several times during his long recitation, Lovey considered escaping to the privy and never coming back. More than once, her cheeks felt so hot she'd have sworn she'd had a hot flash or come down with a fever and might actually faint. It was as if her father could read her mind or that he had some way to know exactly how she'd spent her Friday night while he'd been away. She could hardly look at him as he spoke and instead focused her attention on the floral arrangement in front of the altar.

"Each of these sins is a perversion of something good. And because of the power of sin to corrupt, we must call upon the divine to break us free from its bondage." The passion in his voice rose to a dramatic pitch toward the end of his sermon before he offered his closing remarks and signaled the pianist to begin the altar call. Lovey stopped counting after the third repeat of the same chorus.

She was desperate for someone to be saved, so they could at least move to the lunch portion of their day. Lovey needed some fresh air.

❖

Royal hadn't ridden their family's horse, Midnight, in many days. Sunday morning turned out to be so beautiful that she saddled up the dark mare and made a plan to ride over to Lovey's church in the hopes she'd catch her after the service. She knew today was Decoration Day so she'd use the excuse of bringing flowers to a few distant relatives enjoying their final rest in the grassy, tree-lined cemetery next to the church.

She and Midnight chose a trail away from the main road that led up the ridge from her mother's house and then down an old logging road that would put her out very near the Baptist church.

It was close to one o'clock when she pulled Midnight to a stop under some shady hardwoods and tied her off so that she could nibble some grass. They'd stopped along the way, and as a result, Royal had a handful of wildflowers to leave at the graves.

There was quite a crowd gathered beside a long table, which looked to be where the ladies of the church were laying out all the dishes of food. It took Royal a moment to spot Lovey and then it took Lovey another moment to notice Royal standing at the edge of the church lawn. Royal waved a hello and Lovey walked toward her. It occurred to Royal that this might have been something she should have asked Lovey about before just showing up. They'd never really been together in public except for the occasional encounter at the general store.

She could tell by Lovey's reserved demeanor that she was uncomfortable.

Lovey stopped a respectable distance from Royal.

"What are you doing here?"

"Don't you mean hello?" Royal tried to make a joke because she could tell Lovey was nervous. Damn, why had she been so impulsive and just shown up like this? But the truth was, she knew why. Because she wanted to be part of Lovey's life. Not just her after hours life, but her daytime life too.

"I'm sorry. Yes, I meant to say hello." Lovey smiled, but her posture signaled tension. "You just took me by surprise. I didn't expect to see you here."

Royal revealed the flowers that had been down at her side and Lovey visibly flinched. "Don't worry. These aren't for you. They're for my two great-uncles buried somewhere over there." Royal tipped her chin in the direction of the cemetery.

"Of course." Lovey fidgeted with her hands along the sides of her dress. "Will you stay and eat then?"

Royal was considering whether she should stay or go. This hadn't gone quite like she'd envisioned. "What was the sermon about today?" She thought maybe a little small talk would lighten the mood between them.

"Sins of the flesh."

"You're joking." Royal had made things worse by asking.

"No, I'm not joking. I had to sit quietly and listen for more than an hour about how everything that you and I have done together has damned us both."

Royal swallowed with difficulty, her mouth suddenly dry. "You don't really think that, do you?"

"No, of course not." But the look on Lovey's face was doing little to convince Royal that this was a true statement.

Royal was just about to say something else to try to lighten Lovey's mood when out of nowhere, Joe Dawson showed up.

"Hiya, Royal." He pulled his hat off politely with his greeting.

"Hi, Joe." Royal wasn't sure how to read Lovey's reaction to Joe. She seemed a bit sheepish as she glanced sideways up at Joe.

"Lovey, I have a seat for us in the shade." He smiled down at Lovey. "Come on, this way. See ya later, Royal."

Lovey nodded and allowed herself to be led away by Joe without any remarks to Royal, who stood and watched them walk away in shocked silence. She couldn't help noticing how he placed his hand in a protective way at the small of Lovey's back as they walked back toward the loose array of picnic tables set around the long table with all the food.

Royal placed a hand over her stomach and swayed slightly, suddenly light-headed as a wave of nausea washed up against her.

She knew with certainty she'd just witnessed something she wasn't supposed to see. She'd just seen something Lovey had meant to keep from her. It was as if her view of the world zeroed down to one small circle of light, like a periscope. At the center of that circle was Joe's hand at the small of Lovey's back, and every other peripheral thing went black.

She felt a hand on her arm.

"Royal? You don't look so good. Do you need to sit down?" Laurel Lee, a childhood friend of hers, held out a glass of tea in her direction and had a concerned look on her slender, girlish face.

"Thank you." Royal accepted the cool beverage and took a few sips.

"Come here and sit down." Laurel pulled her toward a bench in the shade and sat next to her. They had a clear view of the table about thirty feet away where Joe and Lovey were seated with others from the congregation.

"You didn't know they were seeing each other, did you?"

"What?" Royal turned to really look at Laurel for the first time. She was focused on the same scene that Royal had been focused on. Why did Laurel care? And then it struck her. Laurel had carried a torch for Joe since probably third grade. She actually wondered why they never got together. Laurel was pretty in a country girl sort of way. She wasn't fancy, she didn't put on airs, but she was kindhearted. Royal had always liked Laurel. Back when school kids made fun of Royal for dressing like a boy, Laurel always took up for her.

Royal slumped back against the bench and took another sip of tea. "How long?"

"It's been a few weeks now. I get the impression it's pretty serious."

Royal leaned forward with her elbows on her knees. She thought she might actually throw up. She felt Laurel's hand on her back.

"It was inevitable. The church ladies have been pushing them together since the day Lovey set foot in Dawsonville." Laurel sighed and leaned back, crossing her arms over her nearly flat chest. "What am I, a loaf of bread? No one ever tried to fix me up with Joe. Why is that? What's Lovey got that I ain't got? Can you tell me that?"

Royal covered her face with her free hand. She couldn't believe this was happening. And if she hadn't shown up unannounced, she still wouldn't know about it. Did Lovey have any intention of telling her that whatever was going on with them didn't mean anything? It was obviously just a temporary thing? Nausea and rage battled inside Royal's knotted stomach.

❖

Lovey tried her best to engage in friendly conversation with those seated around her as Joe filled their plates with food. She wasn't hungry. All she could see was the hurt look on Royal's face. Even from this distance she could tell that Royal was very unhappy and angry. She'd ruined everything and there was no way to fix it right now. She just needed to get through this day and then hope that she could find Royal later and talk with her. Lovey hoped that Royal would leave soon. She'd give anything to know what Laurel was saying to her right now.

In the moment when Joe had walked up to them, she knew she'd handled it badly. She should have told Joe to start without her and taken a moment to speak with Royal. But she'd frozen, knowing that Joe and others in the congregation, including her father, were so nearby. She pinched her nose in an attempt to stave off the headache that was just beginning to rage behind her eyes.

Royal was standing now, pacing in front of the bench and running her fingers through her hair. Lovey prayed that she wouldn't make a scene. *Please don't come over here.*

She felt equal amounts of sadness and relief when she saw Royal climb on her horse and head away from the church. She was called back to the moment by Joe's voice.

"Lovey, aren't you hungry? You've hardly touched your food."

"I guess it's the heat." Lovey smiled weakly and pushed the forgotten food around on her plate.

Sometime later, after the food had been cleared, Lovey noticed one of the deacons talking with her father and her father looked in her direction as if he was displeased with what he was hearing.

Now what? How could this day possibly get any worse?

Well, whatever it was, she wasn't going to wait around to hear about it. She made an excuse to the ladies she was helping clear the tables with and headed toward the privy at the back of the church. She passed by it and kept walking. She'd given her entire day over to others, and *dammit*, she needed to find Royal.

Chapter Twenty-six

Lovey didn't really know where Royal would be, but as she passed by the main square, she saw Midnight tied near a water trough in the shade. That probably meant Royal was in her rented room. Thank heaven for small favors.

She hesitated at the foot of the stairs. What was she going to say to Royal? She'd been rolling several scenarios over in her head during the walk over, and none of them seemed to lead to a happy ending. She took a deep breath. After climbing the stairs to the second floor, heart pounding, Lovey knocked at the door.

"Go away," came the muffled reply.

Lovey deliberated for a moment. She wasn't sure if she should leave until Royal cooled off. No, that would probably just exacerbate things. She knocked again. After a moment, she heard footsteps and then Royal pulled the door open. Her shirt was unbuttoned, revealing her undershirt. And her eyes were red-rimmed. She'd obviously been crying. Lovey's leaden heart sank into her stomach. Royal was hurting, and she was to blame.

"What do you want?" Royal walked back toward the center of the room, leaving Lovey standing at the threshold.

"I want to talk to you." Lovey stepped inside and closed the door. She was afraid her voice was going to break. "I need to talk to you."

"What about?" Royal was obviously very angry so she wasn't going to make this easy for Lovey. Why should she?

"Royal, I know I upset you. I know that whatever you think is going on with Joe and me upset you. Can we please talk about it?"

"Yeah, we can talk about it. Why don't you explain to me what the hell is going on? Laurel said you two have been courting for weeks. Exactly when were you going to tell me? Were you ever going to tell me?"

They were standing awkwardly facing each other in the center of the room. Lovey was suddenly lost to herself. What was she going to say? Had she planned to tell Royal? Probably in some part of her mind she'd believed she could maintain her double life for at least a little bit longer. Before she had to choose between what she thought was *right* and what she *wanted*.

"Royal, I'm so sorry. I never meant for you to find out that way. I never wanted to hurt you." A lump was forming in her throat, and Lovey was having a hard time talking around it.

"So it's true. You are seeing Joe." Royal dropped into the chair near her desk. Her posture defeated.

Lovey stepped close and lifted the partial glass of whiskey that Royal had obviously poured for herself and took a few small sips. The warm liquor helped lessen the lump in her throat. She sat in the upholstered chair opposite Royal.

"Royal, I don't really know what to say to you." She looked around the sparse room for something to focus on besides the crushed look on Royal's face. "Joe is a good man and he has asked me to marry him."

"What?" She could plainly hear the hurt in Royal's voice.

"I haven't said yes yet. I told him I needed some time to think."

"I'd say so. We were only just together Friday night, here in this room. We made love, right here in this bed. Was I the only one who felt something?"

"Royal, you know I feel something for you." She brushed a tear away from her cheek. "I feel something I've never felt before, but we can't really be together, can we? Not the way we want to be. The world doesn't work that way."

"So you're just giving up? You're going to just play by the rules, because you can, because it's easy for you? I can't do that."

"This, what we're doing, it isn't real, Royal. Marriage is a contract, an arrangement. Marriage is what society tolerates. Not this. Not what we're doing."

"I know that deep down you don't believe that, Lovey. It's like you're channeling your father's voice. This…what we have…it *is* real. More real than anything I've ever felt before." Royal placed her open palm over her heart. "This is the only thing that is real."

"What do you expect me to do? Turn my back on my entire life up to this point? Turn away from my father, my faith?"

"If what you're proposing is to live an empty life with someone you're not in love with, then yes, that is what I expect you to do." Royal moved so that she was kneeling in front of Lovey. She held both her hands. "What worth does love or faith hold if it doesn't accept you fully, for who you truly are? That is a false love. A false faith."

Tears started to slowly trail down Lovey's cheeks as Royal spoke to her. Lovey believed that what Royal was saying might be true for her, but Lovey knew she could never go down that path.

"I'm not brave the way you are, Royal."

"Lovey, I'm not brave. I'm in love. With you. Don't do this to us."

"Please don't say that." Lovey wiped at the tears on her cheeks and turned away. She couldn't look at Royal. "Royal, I'm not like you. I care what people think. I can't just be in the world and not notice what people think of me. I don't know how you've managed to not care, but you clearly don't."

"It's not that I don't care what people think, Lovey. But I can't be anyone but who I am. If people don't like me for who I am then they don't really like me and I've got no time for them. Does that make sense?"

"Our worlds are just very different, Royal." Sadness settled over Lovey as if her heart was weighted down with heavy stones. "You've managed to somehow create a life that allows you to be who you truly are, to defy society's conventions of who you should be. I wish I was that strong, but I'm not."

"Lovey, come share my life with me."

"Don't...I can't."

"Lovey, I've never felt for anyone what I feel for you. Please don't let us go."

Lovey shook her head as the tears streamed down her face.

"Lovey, this can be real. If you'll let it be real. We don't have to settle for less. We don't have to live our lives in hiding. You deserve to be whole. We deserve to be whole."

The walls of the room were closing in on Lovey, the air suddenly thick, making it hard for her to breathe. She stood and moved away from Royal's kneeling position. She paced the room, and for a few minutes attempted to visualize a different path.

She pictured herself telling her father that she was in love with Royal. She tried to see the two of them living together, going about their daily lives. She couldn't see it. Everything she attempted to visualize seemed completely incongruent with her experience of the world. She didn't see how it could ever work. Royal was a dreamer, an outlier for whom an unconventional life might work. That sort of path obviously didn't frighten her the way it did Lovey.

She tried to imagine cutting off all ties with her father and the congregation. Even though Lovey disagreed with many of their collective views, there was safety and comfort in blending in. If she married Joe she'd be protected and cared for. His family was supportive and accepting. She knew with Joe she could have what most would define as a good life. No doubt she would grow to love Joe over time. And what she was feeling for Royal would burn out like a shooting star, despite the brilliant light of it across the night sky.

She needed to end this. She was doing neither of them any favors by drawing this out. She knew what she had to do.

"Royal, I'm sorry. We shouldn't see each other anymore." She looked at Royal, who regarded her with a dumbfounded expression on her face. "Believe me when I tell you that this is as hard for me as it is for you, but I'm doing what I believe is best for both of us."

Royal stood up, but didn't speak. She walked across the room running her hand through her hair, her shoulders drooping in defeat.

"You're not doing this for me, Lovey. You're afraid. You're afraid to allow yourself to love me. Don't make this about anything else but what it is. Fear."

"When you've had time to really think this through you'll know I'm right. There's no place here for a love like ours. We have to let it go."

Royal faced Lovey, with a trail of tears on her tanned cheeks. "What if I can't let it go?"

"Royal, you have to. We have to."

"Why?"

"Lots of reasons." Lovey struggled to articulate the jumble of conflicted thoughts in her head. "We would be ostracized if we were to openly declare our love. I'm not ready to bear the weight of that. Are you?"

"For you? Yes. Yes, I am." Royal took a few steps toward her. "Not everyone feels the way you think they do. My family would grow to love you. Don't give up on us before you even try to make it work."

"And if we tried and failed, then the damage would already be done. We couldn't take any of it back. I'd rather stop this before the damage actually happens."

"Don't let fear run your life. Lovey, this doesn't sound like you."

"Maybe you don't know me as well as you think." Self-loathing was settling like a dense fog in her chest. What sort of person hurts the woman they love for a friendly arrangement of marriage? A coward, that's who. She was a coward. Was she? Or was she just being mature and judicious?

She covered her face with her hands. After a minute, she felt the warmth of Royal's hands on her wrists.

"Lovey, please don't do this," whispered Royal. "Give us more time to figure it all out. Just a little more time."

She wanted to sink into Royal's arms. She wanted to cry and say it had all been a horrible mistake. But somewhere, deep inside she heard her father's voice. This was one of those defining moments when a deliberate act was required. Like swallowing a bitter medicine, she knew this was for their own good. If Royal couldn't see that then she would have to see it for both of them.

If she'd known this was going to happen, if she'd known this was going to be the end, would she still have come? Probably not. But here she was, and she knew what she had to do. She felt the conservative paradigm of her entire life constricting around her like a vise, giving her only one choice.

"I can't see you any more, Royal. I'm sorry. I should never have let things go this far."

She waited for Royal to say something, and when she didn't, Lovey let herself out, shutting the door slowly behind her. Her chest seized with heartache as she leaned against the closed door.

She'd never done anything so difficult in her life as walk out of that room. But she knew she had to. She knew that she wasn't ready to love Royal so openly and risk the ridicule of the community. When she said she wasn't brave, she'd meant it. She didn't think she'd be able to withstand the judgment from her father if he ever discovered the truth.

An excruciating pain now would save both of them from the lingering heartache of a world conspiring against them if they tried to be together.

❖

Royal turned around slowly in the center of the room. She was adrift. She knew she should have held some of herself back with Lovey. But she hadn't. And now Lovey had shut the door and carried her heart away.

She slumped back into the chair and was about to take a sip of whiskey when she noticed the faint imprint of Lovey's lipstick on the rim of the glass. Rage surged in her chest. She threw the glass at the door, sending a spray of whiskey and broken shards all over the floor and the wall.

She leaned forward, holding her face in her hands. After a

minute, she couldn't breathe. She stood and began pacing the room from end to end. What was she going to do now? She'd let herself hope. She'd allowed herself to dream.

Dreams were terrible things if you let them take hold, if you truly believed them. A dream could change your world. The death of a dream could destroy it.

❖

An hour or so later, Lovey was walking down the driveway when she saw her father sitting on the porch. She wasn't in the right frame of mind to have a chat with her father so she said hello to him with every intention to breeze past him and go bury her face in her pillow and cry herself to sleep.

"I need to speak with you for a moment, Lovey."

Lovey paused with her hand on the knob of the screen door. She let the door close again and turned toward her father. "Yes?"

"Deacon Wood said something rather disturbing to me after the luncheon today."

She didn't prod him to explain; she just stood stoically watching his face, trying to brace herself for whatever it was he was about to reveal.

"He said that the night of the revival he passed by here and saw a strange car in the driveway. He said the car belonged to Royal Duval." He paused, as if he was waiting for her to say something. When she didn't, he continued. "I told him that he must have been mistaken. I told him that while you had once accepted a ride from Miss Duval that you would not socialize with a woman who was a known moonshine runner and a person of general ill repute."

During her walk back to the house, all Lovey wanted to do was cry; now she found that heavy sadness shifting to anger. She was enraged that some busybody deacon had taken it upon himself to spy on her. In her own house! Despite the fact that this very revelation proved her recent rationale to be true, it still made her angry.

"I invited Royal over for dinner."

"You didn't mention that to me." Her father seemed angry too.

"I'm a grown woman, Father. I didn't think it was necessary to ask your permission to have a friend over for dinner."

"Lovey, I do not want you spending time with Miss Duval. I know you probably feel that your friendship might have a positive influence on her, but I must advise against it."

"Don't worry, Father. I've made it very clear to her that I cannot be her friend." If anything, she'd been a horrible influence on Royal. She'd shown Royal what it meant to be duplicitous and hypocritical.

"Well, I'm relieved to hear it."

"If you don't mind, Father, I'm going to go lie down for a while." She pulled the door open and was inside before he had a chance to respond. She didn't really care what else he had to say. She was emotionally raw and exhausted. She just wanted to hide in her room and wait for the world to go away, or change.

CHAPTER TWENTY-SEVEN

Royal sat in front of the window, trying to write. Nothing was coming to her. She'd started out at the desk, then moved to the bed, and finally had ended up at the window. As it turned out, her position in the room wasn't the problem. She was the problem.

She gave up and headed downstairs and out of the house. She found her grandfather in the barn moving empty glass jars to crates padded with hay for transport later up the trail to the still. Royal joined his effort and then carried some of the crates to the back of the horse drawn wagon.

"You seem really out of sorts lately, Royal. Somethin' you want to talk about?" Her grandfather paused his labor and leaned on the side of the buckboard.

Royal debated whether she wanted to talk about Lovey or not. Before she could decide, her grandfather spoke again.

"Is this about the gal that stopped by the other day? The reverend's daughter?"

Royal stopped shuffling crates and looked at him. "Yeah, I suppose it is." She tried to sound nonchalant when she was actually anything but.

"What happened?"

"I guess I thought we had something going, but she didn't see it that way." She sniffed, determined not to cry in front of her grandfather.

"It's a terrible thing when your happiness depends on another. Sometimes they let you down."

"What do you do about it?" Royal was struggling to feel like herself again. Losing Lovey had rocked her center and completely thrown her. Normally confident and focused, she felt out of balance and unsure of herself. She was miserable. It was as if Lovey had taken the part of her that knew what she wanted and now she was flailing in deep water, as if she forgot how to swim.

"The thing I usually do is remind myself of what makes me happy, and I focus on doing that." Her grandfather pulled a handkerchief free from his pocket and wiped his forehead. The interior of the barn was shaded from the late morning sun, but the temperature was climbing, even in the shade. "In your case, that's driving or writing."

"I haven't been able to write."

"Then driving is where I'd focus." He took a seat on an upturned crate. "Remember the first time I put you behind the wheel of a car?"

Royal's mind traveled back to childhood. She'd pulled herself up as tall as she could on the bench seat beside her grandfather. She had a tiny bit of visibility through the narrow space between the top of the giant steering wheel and the dashboard of the old truck. Golden hay almost as high as the doorknob swished against the steel door of the Model A Ford as Royal and her grandfather had bounced through the back pasture.

Only a month earlier, Royal's father had died in a car accident after tumbling into a ravine. Royal's mother had been upset that this was the time her grandfather had chosen to teach Royal to drive. But Royal had been surly with everyone and listlessly hiding in her room. The suggestion of a driving lesson had been the first time she'd smiled since the funeral. Royal was ten years old.

"Yeah, I remember. It's one of my favorite memories."

"Remember how I told you to listen to the engine? When it got to a certain pitch, if it started to sound like it was straining, you should shift." Her grandfather had leaned over and tapped the speedometer with his finger. She could visualize the scene as if it were yesterday. His teeth were so white against his tanned features every time he smiled down at her. The gearbox had complained loudly when she missed the slot.

"I told you that you couldn't force it." He leaned forward, with his elbows on his knees. "You can't force this either."

"I know."

"She has to find her own way. You can't help her find it. And if you try to force your way on her, it likely won't take."

"I know that too."

Royal walked toward the opening of the barn. She hesitated for a moment in the sun, scuffing the dirt with the toe of her boot. She looked back at her grandfather, partially hidden in shadow, and gave him a halfhearted smile.

"Thanks for talking to me. I think I'll go for a drive."

As she walked toward her car, she called forth again the memory of her first drive with her grandfather. How he'd pulled open the gate and ushered them out on the winding dirt road down the mountain. The feeling of elation she'd had in that moment came rushing back as she settled behind the wheel of her car and cranked the engine. She figured a long drive through the hills would do her some good. She eased onto the dirt road and headed north, into the mountains.

❖

Lovey lifted several garments and inspected them for rips or tears. She and a few other women from the church were sorting donated clothing that would end up being delivered to the children's home in Gainesville. The task today was to repair any small imperfections, like rips or missing buttons, before delivering the garments for dispersal to needy kids. She held up a tiny dress and felt a pang that she and George had not had a chance to have a child. If they'd had a child, at least she wouldn't feel so alone.

As soon as she formulated the thought, she realized her loneliness was her own choice. She'd not felt alone with Royal, but because of her own fears, she'd pushed Royal away. She let her hands, holding the small pink dress, drop to a heap in her lap and gazed down at it.

"Are you all right, Miss Lovey?" She heard a young woman's voice and looked up to see Laurel Lee regarding her.

"I'm fine." She remembered that Laurel was the woman she'd seen with Royal that day at the church when everything had gone so wrong. She'd wondered ever since that day what Laurel and Royal had talked about. But how could she ask? She didn't know Laurel except distantly as a fellow church member. They'd never spoken more than a few words to each other. And to question her about Royal would likely only give the gossip mill fuel.

Or was she so self-involved that she just thought everyone cared about what she was up to when in fact, no one was paying attention? She wasn't sure.

"So, you and Joe Dawson seem to be getting along." It was a statement more than a question from Laurel. It seemed she wanted to connect with Lovey in some way. Maybe because they were the only two at the church this morning who were close to the same age. The rest of the women, clustered near a large pile of clothes they were sorting, were much older.

"Yes, we are." Lovey wasn't sure how much she wanted to reveal to Laurel about Joe. She didn't really want to talk about Joe. She was dying to ask about Royal. She decided to tread lightly and see what she could uncover. "I saw you speaking with Royal Duval the other day after the service. Are you two friends?"

Laurel seemed to smile with satisfaction. Maybe she wasn't the only one looking for an opportunity to talk about Royal. Lovey's stomach knotted as she waited for Laurel to respond.

"I've known Royal since we were kids. She's a real character, that Royal. She definitely marches to the beat of her own drum, if you know what I mean."

Lovey was trying to discern judgment from Laurel's comment, but she didn't hear reproach in Laurel's voice, only playfulness.

"I do think I know what you mean."

Lovey tried to envision Royal as a youngster. She pictured a towheaded child, dressed like a boy, playful and carefree. She contrasted that against her own experience as a child. She could call forth the feelings she'd had as a young girl, seated quietly on a hard church pew, listening to her father in the pulpit. There had been no tolerance for distraction or fidgeting. *Sit up straight. Shoulders back. Be seen and not heard.* And all the other admonishments little girls endured so that they would grow up to be the Southern belles their parents desired.

Lovey ached to share her true feelings with someone, but she didn't know Laurel well enough to know whether she could be trusted.

"She was pretty upset about you and Joe." And there it was. Laurel had made the first genuine move toward honesty.

Lovey looked down at her hands in her lap trying to decide how much to say. Her emotions were so raw, so near the surface, that she feared even trying to share the smallest amount of her true feelings would cause the dam to burst and she'd lose total control. The last thing she wanted was to dissolve into a crying heap on the floor of the fellowship hall.

"She was upset?" That was lame, but she wanted Laurel to share more.

"Yeah, I don't think she knew you and Joe were seeing each other. It's a terrible thing to see the person you care about with someone else."

A knot formed quickly in Lovey's throat, and she knew there were tears in her eyes when she looked at Laurel. "I was—" The words died as her voice was choked by tears. She stood abruptly and went to sit in one of the small Sunday school rooms off the main fellowship hall.

She was crouched into one of the tiny kid-sized chairs when she felt Laurel settle into the seat beside her. "I'm sorry. I didn't mean to upset you."

Lovey shook her head. "It's not your fault."

"There now, there ain't nothin' that can't be fixed here. Why don't you just go talk to Royal?"

Lovey shook her head again. "I can't. She'd never speak to me after the things I've said to her." She leaned back and let out a long sigh. There. She'd finally said something real about what she was feeling. She drew in a shaky breath.

"You don't know that until you try."

"Why are you so interested in what's going on with me and Royal?"

"I have my reasons." Laurel smiled and patted Lovey's arm. "I have my reasons."

CHAPTER TWENTY-EIGHT

It was probably past midnight when Royal stepped out of the car and walked toward Frank Mosby and a small group that gathered around Mason's car. Ned exited the passenger side and followed along on her heels.

"I figured you wouldn't show, Royal," Mason yelled in her direction.

"And here I figured you for the no-show," Royal yelled back at him. She took another sip from the flask she had in her jacket pocket.

Mason Griggs was a regulation asshole. He spent weekends at his grandparents' place outside of Dawsonville. His daddy had money, and Mason made sure everyone knew what a glamorous, exciting life he led in Atlanta. He loved rubbing everyone's face in it whenever possible, tonight being no exception.

"Royal, don't do this. You've got nothing to prove to this jackass." Ned was leaning into her, talking to her in hushed tones.

"I've got this, Ned." She brushed him off. "It's time someone put him in his place. And I'm in just the mood to do it."

Royal approached the small cluster of folks with Ned trailing on her heels.

"We run wide-open. The first one to the turn wins." Mason had been drinking also. His words were a little slurred.

"What do I win?" Royal needed just a bit more motivation than putting Mason in his place. She decided she wanted a trophy, a reward of some kind.

"Whoever wins gets a date with me." Vonda Harris draped her arm over Mason's shoulder with flirtatious flair.

Royal took another swig from her flask. Vonda Harris loved to pop a cork and had a reputation for going around with lots of boys. She was pretty, but not the settling down type.

"I could show you a thing or two, Royal Duval. And I'd have a good time doin' it." Vonda twirled a finger in Royal's direction as she hung on Mason's shoulder. The low-cut opening of her dress dipped low to reveal a distracting view of her cleavage.

Royal winked at Vonda. "I might just show you somethin', Vonda." She took one more sip of whiskey before she turned toward her car. She pulled her car up in line with Mason's.

"I'll start you off," Frank offered.

The car bumpers were lined up with each other on either side of the dirt road. Royal depressed the accelerator and her V-8 roared.

Mason cranked up the car his daddy had recently purchased for him. It was a tan roadster with a ragtop. It was also equipped with a V-8 but without the special modifications that Ned had made to Royal's.

Royal figured fair was fair. He didn't ask and she didn't offer. Everyone knew she was the better driver. He was stupid to call her out.

Ned leaned into the driver's side window. "Royal, don't do this. You've been drinkin' and you're just being bullheaded. Don't let your hurt feelings over Lovey make you do stupid things."

Royal shoved Ned's arm out of the window. "Shut up, Ned. This has got nothing to do with Lovey. Just go stand on the sidelines like you always do."

She saw the hurt look on Ned's face, but she didn't care. She was in a bad mood, and driving fast and showing the insufferable Mason Griggs who was the better driver would be the only cure for her ill temper.

Frank stood between the two cars with raised arms. A few other onlookers, including Vonda, stood on either shoulder to watch. Both drivers revved their engines.

"Ready! Set! Go!" As he shouted *go*, Frank dropped his arms, and the two cars lurched past him in a cloud of dust.

The heavy Ford blasted down the straightaway, pulling ahead of Mason's roadster. Royal white-knuckled the steering wheel as she fought to pull ahead of the other car. Visions of Lovey flashed through her mind and anger knotted in her chest. It had been two weeks since she'd seen Lovey, and with every passing day, the hurt of it just kept expanding. She felt the sadness of their breakup like a creeping web of cancer spreading to her bones.

Distracted momentarily, she realized she'd let Mason slip up on her. She gave the Ford some gas, but Mason matched her speed. Then, without warning, he swerved into her. She glanced over at him, but he seemed to be struggling with the weighty car at such a great speed. He bounced into her again, and this time the right front tire of her car caught a ridge of raised dirt at the shoulder, and she realized she was going off the road.

A tree flashed in her headlights just a split second after the car left the roadway, over the shoulder and slammed at full speed into the base of a gnarled, leafless oak. Her forehead cracked loudly against the steering wheel; blackness enveloped her senses.

❖

Days and days had passed with no word from Royal. Lovey wasn't sure what she'd expected. Did she think Royal would pursue her? She'd made it pretty clear what she was going to do. She'd left Royal with every impression that she would accept Joe's marriage proposal and that they should both move on with their lives.

Joe had been very attentive to her since he'd popped the question, no doubt expecting her response to be yes. Lovey cared for Joe, but she knew he did not fulfill her. Lulled by the familiar, she lapsed into vague discontent. Joe made her feel safe, but unsatisfied, which somehow made her not feel safe at all. Had she made a terrible mistake?

On days when she felt particularly sad, she carried Royal's

borrowed handkerchief in her skirt pocket. The soft linen square reminded her of the only time she'd known for sure she was truly happy. She held the fabric to her face and was transported far away.

She was doing just that one morning at the kitchen table when Cal interrupted her thoughts.

"Are you all right, Miss Lovey?"

"What?" Lovey was a bit startled. She'd been so lost in her own mental wonderings that she hadn't heard Cal come in. "I'm fine."

"I know it ain't none of my business, but you seem real sad lately. I worry about you."

"You shouldn't worry. I'm fine."

"Can I make you something to eat?" Cal regarded her with a tender expression on her face.

"I'm not hungry, but thank you, Cal. It's kind of you to offer." She was sure that Cal noticed the handkerchief with Royal's monogram on it. She'd forgotten to hide it from view.

"Are you and Royal not friends anymore?"

For a moment, Lovey was at a loss for words. No one besides Laurel had asked about Royal. She didn't even know how Cal knew to ask. Maybe she and Grace were friends and Grace had mentioned it.

"I'm not sure what we are anymore, Cal." She gave Cal the first honest answer she'd given anyone lately. She was a shell of her former self, falling back on her practiced behavior as a preacher's daughter of saying only what she was supposed to and doing only what was expected of her. Emptiness surrounded her like a cloud. This was worse than losing George, which she'd had no control over. She'd brought this on herself. She'd chosen in direct conflict with her own desires and she was miserable because of it.

"I think Royal is having a hard time too." Cal fidgeted sheepishly, rubbing her hands together in front of her plump frame as if she wasn't sure she should be saying what she was saying.

"What do you mean?" Lovey wanted to know and didn't want to know at the same time. Not knowing certainly wasn't keeping her from thinking about Royal anyway.

"She's been acting a little crazy. Drinking more. She wrecked her car."

"She wrecked her car? What happened?" Fear seized Lovey's chest like a vise at the thought of Royal, hurt, and her nowhere close by to help.

"Grace said Sam told her that Royal was drag racing and run through a ditch and into a tree. She hasn't been able to drive for work. Ned and Sam have been tryin' to fix the car." She paused for a moment as if gathering her thoughts. "Royal is a right mess if you ask me. She's gonna get herself killed if she don't snap out of it."

"Was she hurt?"

"She just banged her hard head." Cal began to put away the groceries she'd carried in. "Maybe you should go see her, Miss Lovey. You might be the only one who could talk any sense into that crazy head of hers."

"I don't think that's such a good idea, Cal." So Grace knew that she and Royal had been involved in some way. Apparently, so did Sam and now Cal. She felt a little exposed, but not judged. She excused herself and moved to the porch.

In another few weeks she'd begin her teaching appointment. She had always enjoyed teaching, but she was dreading it now. Seeing the hopeful faces of children look up at her for inspiration would just make all of it worse. Would it be as easy to lie to them as it was to lie to herself?

CHAPTER TWENTY-NINE

Royal leaned on the hood of the old Model A Ford truck. "What do you mean I'm not driving?"

"I'm taking this load myself. You've been reckless lately, and I don't need you on this run." Wade hauled the last crate to the truck bed and pulled the tarp over it. "Whatever is going on with you, Royal, figure it out. Until then, you've got no car and you sure aren't driving this one."

She leaned back and shoved her hands in her pockets. "Fine." She said the word, but she knew she was anything but fine. Royal was rattled and off her game. Ever since the night she'd wrecked her car she'd been a mess. Hell, she'd been a hot mess ever since Lovey walked out of her life. And now she'd given Wade the perfect window to cut her out of the one thing she liked doing. Driving.

He was up to something. He never wanted to drive before. She was suspicious that something else was going on and that her recent behavior was a convenient excuse.

Royal stepped back out of the way as Wade pulled the heavy truck through the wide barn door. Dust billowed behind the dark auto as he gave it gas and headed down the dirt drive to the main road.

There was an old wooden crate nearby, and after she watched the taillights fade, she turned around and put her boot through the wood slats. Then she picked up the splintered remnants and slammed it against the wall. She was looking for something else to destroy when she heard her grandfather's voice behind her.

"Hey, now! What are you doin'?"

Royal turned on her heel, breathing hard. "Nothin'."

"It didn't look like nothin' to me." He moved to the opening of the barn door, moonlight reflecting on his face. He must have come through the door at the back of the stalls, but Royal was making so much noise during her fit of rage that she hadn't heard him.

"You need to deal with this anger before it gets you in trouble."

"I'm dealing with it."

"Well, I'm here if you need to talk."

"Thanks." The last thing Royal wanted to do was talk. She was angry and on edge. It was past nine, and Royal needed to be anywhere but here. She decided to walk into town for a drink. Maybe if Ned were around he'd be up for a drink too.

"I'm gonna walk into town. I'll see you later." Royal waved a hand at her grandfather as she strode toward Ned's house in the dark.

❖

The Mill was a cacophony of loud male voices and piano music when they arrived. Ned followed Royal to the rough, wide plank bar, and she ordered them both a drink. Whiskey for her and a beer for Ned.

Royal leaned back against the bar and scanned the smoky room. She saw some faces she recognized and some she didn't. There were a few women scattered about the room, protectively hovering next to their men. As if Royal would ever even look at a woman again. Could any creature be more hurtful than a woman? She didn't think so. And it would be a frosty morning in hell before she ever trusted her heart to another one.

She drained her glass and banged it on the bar, signaling for a refill.

"Hey, slow down there, Royal. If you get too drunk you know I can't carry you home."

"Don't mother me, Ned. I know my limits."

"Yeah, the other night you knew your limits all the way into that oak tree."

"Shut up, Ned." Royal watched as June approached from the other end of the bar with a half-full bottle.

"You okay, Royal? Why don't you go easy on this tonight?" June gave Royal a concerned matronly once-over.

"Don't you start mothering me too, June. I already got one mother and his name is Ned." She patted Ned's shoulder and she and June shared a laugh.

"I ain't laughin', Royal." Ned stewed over his beer.

She was just about to take a sip from her freshly filled glass when she felt a hand on her shoulder. Joe Dawson. *Fuck you, Joe Dawson* were the first words that came to mind. Luckily, she didn't say them out loud. Wasn't it enough that the whole damn county carried his family name? Wasn't it enough that he'd stolen Lovey right out from under her damn nose? She postponed her next sip, setting the glass on the bar and turning to face him. Ned, who'd only been partially aware of all that had been going on between Royal and Lovey, stiffened beside her protectively.

"I need a word with you, Royal." Joe had obviously gotten quite a head start on her in the drinks department. His speech was almost slurred.

"Thanks, but no thanks. Shove off, Joe." She turned her back to Joe, resting her elbows on the bar, her boot propped on the railing along the front.

"I need to have a word with you. I ain't kiddin', Royal." He put his hand on her shoulder again, and before she could turn and take a swing at him, Ned slid his slender frame between them.

"Come on now, Joe. I don't know what's up, but why don't we just settle down here? I don't think Royal's in the mood to talk." Ned held both of his open palms in front of him as a sign of non-aggression. He would have physically been no match for Joe's muscle mass and height anyway.

"It's okay, Ned. I'll handle this." Royal downed the remaining brown liquor in her glass and motioned with a jerk of her head for Joe to join her outside.

Ned whispered urgently as he followed her out the door.

"Royal, don't do this. Let's just keep walkin' and go home." He tried to grab at her arm, but she pulled away, barely able to contain the anger she'd been carrying inside for weeks.

"Go home if you want to, Ned. This doesn't have anything to do with you anyway."

Ned followed Royal out to the alley behind the Mill where she turned to face Joe. "So what's so important that you have to talk to me right now about it?"

"I don't want you hanging around Lovey. I know what you're up to, Royal Duval, and I'm here to tell you that Lovey is my intended and I don't want you anywhere near her!" Joe jabbed his index finger in the direction of her face as he spoke.

Well, clearly Joe wasn't up on current events and didn't know that Lovey had already given Royal the heave-ho. For some reason, Joe still believed that Royal held some threat to his relationship with Lovey. That was an interesting bit of news, but likely false.

Royal was angry on so many levels she didn't know which to tap into first. That Joe had the nerve to say anything to her about Lovey when he'd clearly already won that fight, made her angry. But equally galling was the fact that he thought he could tell her who she could and couldn't spend time with in the first place. What an arrogant asshole. She would choose her own friends, by God.

"Joe Dawson, you don't tell me how to spend my time or who to spend it with. I'll socialize with who I damn well please."

"Royal, don't test me. I'm serious. You stay away from Lovey."

Royal shoved him with both hands. "Make me."

"Don't make me hit you, Royal, 'cause I will."

Even in the low light from the gas lamp overhead, Royal could tell Joe's face was flushed. He was angry too and trying to hold back. So of course she shoved him again. Part of her wanted him to fight. At least then she'd have some physical outlet for the rage and hurt she was feeling. And he was the perfect target because all of it was his fault.

Joe shoved her backward. She stumbled but then ran toward him, jumping on him and causing him to fall backward. She punched him once, twice in the jaw before he grabbed her by the shirt and threw her off.

He was so much bigger and stronger than she was. He got to his feet and had Royal in a headlock trying to spin her around while she attempted to land a few blows to his ribs. They were both winded and stirring up dust. And then something else happened.

Two other fellows had stepped into the alley, and Royal just caught a glimpse of them headed her way with a wooden club when she saw Ned intervene.

"Stop! Joe, let me go!" She was trying to break free before the two men descended on Ned, but Joe was too drunk and his reflexes were slow. Plus, his back was turned toward Ned so he couldn't see what was happening.

Royal saw the one man swing and hit Ned in the side of the head, sending him backward so that he landed against the edge of the raised porch of the Mill.

Royal pushed furiously against Joe just as the man raised the club to swing at Joe. Joe still had one arm around Royal but released her as he blocked the blow with his other arm, then turned and landed a solid left hook under the man's chin, sending him to the ground.

Royal pushed past the second fellow to where Ned lay motionless on the ground.

"Ned! Ned!" She dropped to her knees beside him.

His eyes were open, but he was deathly still. She tentatively touched the back of his head, and when she pulled her hand away it was covered with blood. Tears filled her eyes as she turned to look back at Joe. He was holding the wooden rod in one hand and the man by the front of his shirt in the other.

All at once, Royal's foggy brain called forth the memory of these men. They were two of the men who tried to assault Grace that night. They'd obviously come back to settle the score with Royal and instead Ned had gotten in their way.

"Royal? Is Ned—?" Joe held the squirming man firmly as he spoke.

Royal shook her head as tears began to slide down her cheeks.

The second man who'd been standing nearby finally spoke.

"We didn't mean no harm to the boy. It were an accident. We didn't mean no harm." He lingered for a moment and then took off running, leaving his friend behind.

"Help! Help! We need a doctor out here!" Joe was yelling as he pinned the other man against the wall. He was the one who had swung at Ned, and Joe held on to him.

Royal pressed Ned's limp hand against her cheek. This was all her fault. All her stupid, stubborn, prideful fault.

"Oh, Ned, don't do this. This can't be happening." She laid her ear on his heart, but she heard nothing.

A couple of people from inside the tavern now appeared at the entrance to the alley as a result of Joe's shouted requests for help. One of them knelt next to Ned and felt for a pulse. The other went to assist Joe with the struggling culprit. Then more people came. Gentle hands pulled Royal away from Ned's body as several men lifted him into the back of a car.

"They're gonna take him to Doc's place, Royal." June pulled Royal along with an arm around her shoulders. "Come inside, honey. There's nothing you can do for Ned now."

Royal looked back as Ned's lifeless body was carried to a waiting car and laid across the backseat. His head bobbed limply to one side, and someone gently turned it so the car door would shut. June half carried her back inside as the car carrying Ned pulled away.

CHAPTER THIRTY

Lovey saw the postman's carriage pause near the end of their drive before proceeding. Maybe she'd gotten a letter from Dottie. She'd been missing her friend and longed to catch up with her. Things were going well for Dottie, and Lovey wouldn't mind basking in the glow of her good fortune for a little while. Even from a distance.

When she reached the post, she saw that there was a letter addressed to her with no return address. The handwriting looked somewhat familiar, and the moment she opened the envelope she knew it was from Royal. She unfolded the ivory paper and turned it over in her hand. There was no note, despite the fact that the name on the envelope had been hers. A single poem had been typed, centered on the page:

Desire's flame burns my skin
I long for the relief
Only your lips can bring
My body holds a space for you.

Released
Through your window
Into darkness and stiff shrubs
Crossing the dew-laden lawn in sock feet.

Now, settled in my car
I try to imagine my future without you.
I can't.
I won't.

What resides in my chest is real
Set against the relentless unreal.
Defying convention.

Only an unfeeling world refuses
To see what we have seen.
Brilliant. Iridescent. Eternal.
Love.

Her hand began to shake so that she could no longer make out the words. Lovey covered her mouth with her other hand as she began to sob silently. Why would Royal send such a poem except to torment her? Did Royal not realize the impact sentiments such as this would have on her?

She folded the letter and shoved it in her pocket.

For a moment, she struggled with what to do. Tightness in her chest made it hard for her to catch her breath. She thought if she walked back into the house she might suffocate.

Lovey began to walk down the road, taking deep breaths, willing the sobs to subside. She was almost to the curve where she'd met Royal that first night before she realized how far she'd gotten. The memory of that night started the sobs again.

She stepped off the road and stumbled down to the edge of the pond where Royal had tended to her bee stings on a blanket spread on the grass. She dropped to the ground, lay on her side, pulled her knees up to her chest, and cried. She had not given herself permission to fully grieve, but now that she'd gone over the edge, she was lost in the sea of it. Her sorrow washed over her again and again like waves on a shoreline.

She wasn't sure how long she lay in the grass. At one point she rolled onto her back and watched the sun's rays pass through the broad poplar leaves swaying in the breeze above her.

Eventually, her emotions settled enough that she thought she could face returning to the house. She saw her father enter the house ahead of her and was struck by how much she'd agreed to settle for this life. Even though this was not the life she'd envisioned for herself. And even as she realized this, she knew that only she could change the course her life had taken.

CHAPTER THIRTY-ONE

Lovey was still in terrible spirits two days later when Joe stopped by to sit with her on the porch. He seemed oddly quiet. It was just as well because she had decided to break things off with Joe. She was miserable, and she guessed that she must be making Joe miserable, although he hadn't said as much.

She might as well just be alone. If she couldn't have what she wanted, the person she truly desired, then she would rather have no one. She would rather be alone.

She was getting ready to say something to Joe when he spoke first.

"Something terrible has happened, Lovey." He held his hat in his hand as he sat beside her on the rocker.

A small table between them held a pitcher of lemonade that she'd carried out just after he arrived. She set her glass there and looked at Joe. She really looked at him. He was obviously burdened with something, and she'd been too distracted with her own melancholy to notice.

"What is it, Joe?"

"Two nights ago, at the Mill…there was a terrible accident."

Lovey's already unsettled stomach churned. *Oh God, please don't say something happened to Royal.* She waited for him to continue as her mind raced ahead to think the worst.

"Royal and I got into a fight and—"

"You hurt Royal?" The pitch of Lovey's voice went up an octave.

"No, but there were two other men, and Royal and I were wrestling and we didn't see them coming. But Ned did and he stepped in front of them."

"Joe, what happened?" Lovey's heart pounded in her chest and in her ears like thunder.

"Ned was killed. One of the fellas had a wooden club. He was about to swing at us, but Ned caught him first. The blow knocked him back, and when he fell he hit the edge of the raised porch. The fall broke his neck."

Lovey covered her mouth with her hand, horrified. Royal must be crushed.

"I guess these fellas had tried to hurt Grace Watkins before and Royal had stopped them so two of them had come back to get even with her, only they hadn't counted on Ned or me."

"Oh my God. This is terrible." In her shock, Lovey continued speaking without remembering to filter what she was saying. "I was with Royal that night. The night she stopped those men from hurting Grace."

As soon as she spoke, she realized she'd revealed more to Joe than she'd intended. She looked over at him and couldn't quite discern his reaction. He didn't seem surprised.

"Lovey, I know something happened between you and Royal."

"How—"

"Laurel Lee told me. She knew the day that Royal came to the church lunch."

Lovey didn't know what to say. She studied her hands folded in her lap. She waited for Joe to become angry. She waited for the words of recrimination to come, but they never came. Instead of reproach, his words only carried kindness.

"If I hadn't called Royal out to tell her to stay away from you, then Ned might still be alive. I shouldn't have tried to control things. I should have listened to my own heart."

Lovey felt tears gathering around her lashes. "And what does your heart tell you, Joe?"

"It tells me that you're in love with someone else and that I need to let you go." A tear slowly trailed down his unshaven cheek, and Lovey brushed it away with her fingers.

"Oh, Joe." She took his hand in hers, feeling truly connected to him for maybe the first time. "I never meant to lead you on or be dishonest. I just…"

"I know, Lovey. The world ain't always fair. But you can't help who you love. And right now, Royal needs you." He brushed at another tear as it fell. "I couldn't live with myself if I didn't say this to you and try to make things right." He stood abruptly. Lovey stood also and pulled him into a hug.

"Where is she?"

"The funeral was gonna be this afternoon. I'm guessing she's at the cemetery up at the Hill Church." Joe stepped off the porch and pulled on his hat. It had started to rain. "I can take you there in the buggy if you want."

Lovey nodded and without hesitation followed Joe to his carriage and climbed aboard.

❖

The mourners had come and gone. Standing in the rain under a darkened sky in their black clothing, her uncle had stared her down with his silent rage. She knew he'd wished she was in the pine box, under the dark earth instead of Ned.

Her mother had been the last to leave Royal's side. She'd taken Teddy home to meet others at the house who were bringing food and anything else they could that might provide some comfort, but there was no comfort.

The preacher had said the things he knew he should say. The things people expected to hear on a day such as this. That mankind in our smallness cannot know the mind of God in workings such as these. That we must all trust in the Lord's divine plan for our lives even when things seem terrible or unfair.

How could Ned's death be God's will?

This was nothing more than accidental chaos inflicted on the innocent. With Royal lay all the blame. She should never have started a fight with Joe. She should have listened to Ned. She should have let Lovey go and moved on. She'd pulled everyone down with her grief, and Ned had paid the ultimate price.

Royal stood rock still in her black suit at the gravesite, letting the rain flood her senses. The previously sun-warmed, freshly turned earthen mound beneath which her cousin Ned took his final rest was steaming in the cool, summer shower. She studied the dark earth, watching small rivulets develop and run along the raised mound. She clenched and unclenched her fists. She silently recited a poem she'd written. Words she'd been carrying since Ned's fateful fall.

The end of all things comes swiftly
Without warning
Without empathy
Cold, black, nothingness arrives complete.

Others left to feel the absence
That I will not perceive
I am no more
All that might have been, abandoned.

Everlasting nothing
Moonless midnight
Selfless at last
All my worries forgotten, forevermore.

She didn't want to leave Ned alone. She was the last witness to remain at the site of his eternal sleep and found herself unable to walk away.

❖

Lovey hugged Joe and thanked him before she stepped out of the buggy.

"Do you want me to wait?"

"No, you've done enough. Thank you, Joe."

He touched his hat and snapped the reins, leaving her standing in the rain to look for Royal. The funeral must be over. Only Royal's car remained, a car with a dented front fender and broken headlight, and a single bullet hole. Royal had to be here somewhere.

After searching for a few moments, she found Royal lingering by the fresh grave, rain soaked and forlorn. Lovey stepped close, but Royal didn't seem to notice her.

Grace and Sam stood twenty feet away or so, under a black umbrella. Silent sentinels bearing witness to Royal's grief from a respectful distance.

Lovey reached out and touched Royal's face with her fingers and only then did Royal turn and notice her presence. Her eyes were dark and clouded with grief. Her long lashes laden with raindrops.

"Come with me, baby," Lovey whispered to her, caressing her cheek softly. She took Royal's arm, and as they turned toward the car, she nodded to Grace and Sam as if to say, *I'll take care of her.*

Lovey opened the door of the black Ford and waited until Royal was settled before she circled the front of the car and climbed into the driver's seat. The keys were still in the ignition. She cranked the car and eased the heavy auto off the soggy grass back onto the muddy unpaved road.

Royal slumped against the window. Raindrops streamed down the glass past her reflection. If she was surprised to see Lovey, it did not register on her face. They rode in silence as Lovey drove them back into town. After parking out of sight behind the tavern, she took Royal's hand and they solemnly climbed the stairs to Royal's place hand in hand.

Once behind the locked door, Lovey stepped close to Royal. She slipped her hands inside Royal's dark, sopping wet suit coat and eased it off her shoulders, hanging it on the back of a nearby chair. Then she took a towel off the stand near the basin and began to gently dry Royal's hair. Royal seemed lost. She didn't speak, and she made no move to assist Lovey with her task. Her face was wet with rain or tears or both. Lovey's damp dress clung to her body, causing her to shiver. But she needed to tend to Royal first.

Lovey kissed her cheek and whispered, "Let's get you out of these drenched things."

As Lovey began to unbutton the sagging starched white shirt, Royal covered her eyes with the palms of her hands and sobbed quietly. There was no sound, only the shaking of her shoulders. Lovey pulled Royal's hands away from her face, dabbing at the tears with the towel, and then shifted Royal's arms so that she could remove the wet shirt. There was a damp undershirt to pull over Royal's head before she was bare chested in front of Lovey.

She saw that Royal had bruises on her forehead and around one eye. She wondered if that was from hitting the tree with her car or from the fight with Joe. She traced a fingertip around the outside edge of the bruises.

Lovey softly stroked Royal's arms. She pulled Royal close and kissed her along her jawline and then down her neck. "I'm so sorry," she whispered against Royal's neck.

"What are you doing here?" Royal's voice was hoarse with emotion.

"I knew you needed me. Oh, Royal, I'm so sorry about Ned. I'm so sorry about everything."

Righteous anger had allowed Royal to create distance between them, but underneath her rage lurked a heavy unrequited want, a need to be known, a need to be held by Lovey. Royal knew a touch would be all it would take. One brush of Lovey's fingertips in just the right spot and Royal knew she would burst into flame for her. She wanted to be wholly consumed, to bury herself in the depths of her. She stood at the edge of darkest grief. Did Lovey sense her longings?

She stood silently as Lovey unfastened her belt and trousers. Royal stepped out of the rest of her clothing, and Lovey ushered her to the bed and under the covers. She looked up at Lovey, waiting for what might happen next.

After a few minutes of silent deliberation, Lovey pulled off her wet things and climbed under the covers next to Royal. Her skin was smooth but cool to the touch because of the chill of the rain and standing for too long in damp clothing.

Lovey propped herself up on one elbow, and with her other hand, stroked Royal's face and down the center of her chest. She sweetly kissed Royal on the cheek.

"Lovey, I've missed you so terribly."

"I know, baby. I've missed you too."

Lovey had never used that term of endearment for Royal, and just the sound of it sweetly uttered and meant for her caused a tear to rise and roll slowly down her cheek.

Royal pulled Lovey into a long, deep kiss that led to further exploration. Royal found that it wasn't within her power to hold anything back with Lovey. She figured she'd regret all of this in the morning, but right now, in the fading hours of daylight, she was powerless to do anything else. She gave herself over fully to the moment.

She rolled on top of Lovey and set upon her with furious passion. She wanted to possess Lovey's pale, perfect form from head to toe and every tender place in between. She focused her touch, her thrusts in such a way that Lovey called her name as she climaxed in Royal's arms. Royal held her close, placing tender kisses on her forehead and on her lips. Her sadness momentarily soothed, Royal settled against Lovey, with her cheek on Lovey's shoulder. Lovey stroked her hair and whispered softly that everything would be okay now.

Would it? How could Lovey know for sure?

CHAPTER THIRTY-TWO

Lovey became aware of her surroundings slowly, as if rising from under water. Once she was awake she realized it was foggy out. Overcast, but not raining. She realized she was alone in Royal's bed. She'd slept so soundly after they made love. Maybe more soundly than she'd slept in weeks. She sat up, rubbing the sleep from her eyes, allowing the sheet to fall to her waist. Only then did she notice the handwritten note on the pillow beside her.

> *Dearest Lovey,*
>
> *Last night may have saved my life. I know I cannot ask for more. I know that what we had cannot exist in the light of day, but for the small reminder of how wonderful life could be if...only if. Thank you.*
>
> *I do still love you and I hope that you find what you need with Joe.*
>
> *—Royal*

Oh, no. No. No. No. Royal still thinks Joe and I are together. Lovey realized that they hadn't talked. Royal had no idea that she and Joe had broken things off. What time was it and where was Royal now?

Lovey put her head in her hands. How had this happened? If only Royal had woken her up before she left. They could have talked everything out. Not only did she still need to make things right with Royal, she'd left her home for the entire night. Her father would no doubt be beside himself with worry and anger. She'd have to face that when she got home too. On some level she realized that action alone had probably started a chain reaction that she would have to deal with.

She dressed quickly, splashed some water on her face from the basin, and after stopping in the bathroom down the hall from Royal's room, briskly walked toward home. It was a cool morning. Fog hung in the air from the previous day's rain, and heavy droplets fell from broad-leafed poplars. The dripping water almost made it seem as if it was raining again as she walked to her house. During her walk, she'd devised a plan. She would freshen up, change clothes, borrow the car, and go find Royal.

As she drew near to the house, she saw that there was a dark sedan in the driveway. She walked past the car that bore a single light on its roof. Boyd Cotton. That's where she'd seen this car before. This didn't seem right. What was he doing here?

She crept to the front porch and listened for voices from inside the house. Boyd and her father obviously thought no one else was around so there was no point keeping their voices low. It was easy to overhear what they were saying through the screen door. Lovey stood just out of sight and listened.

"We've booked the delivery for tonight. And it's a big one," said Boyd.

"And you're sure they'll be transporting enough to require arrest? This whole scheme only matters to me if we can shut them down." That was her father's voice now.

"Trust me on this. I've seen to it. An order this big will carry jail time for sure." She could hear Boyd skid the chair on the hardwood floor. He must be about to leave. "Then you get your dry county and I get Wade. He's crossed me for the last time. Everybody wins."

Lovey was confused. Why would her father be involved with local law enforcement? She heard footsteps so she quickly jumped off the porch so that she could pretend she was just walking up as Boyd exited.

"Why, Mrs. Porter. Nice to see you again." Boyd resettled his broad-brimmed hat and then tipped it in her direction.

"Sheriff Cotton." She nodded her acknowledgment of him.

"Y'all have a good day now. I think the sun will come out shortly." Boyd looked up at the sky, tossed his hat onto the passenger seat, and waved as he backed out of the still muddy driveway.

Lovey watched him leave then turned to see that her father had been watching her from the door he held open. The look on his face was the epitome of parental disapproval, and she was in no mood for it.

She gave him an equally disapproving look as she brushed past him into the house. In the kitchen she saw that there was a county map spread on the table with markings on it. She wasn't familiar enough with the area to sort out locations before her father caught up to her and pulled the map away and rolled it up.

"What's going on?" Lovey was uncharacteristically direct with her father. "Why was Boyd Cotton here at the house? What could you possibly have to talk with him about?" She couldn't help herself. She asked questions in rapid succession.

"What I need to know is where you were last night, young lady? I'll do the asking."

"I was with Royal. Did you know her cousin Ned was killed?"

"I did know. The unfortunate end to a life of low character."

Lovey ignored the slur against Ned. "What were you talking to Boyd about? What delivery has been booked?"

Her father visibly stiffened. "Drinking alcohol is unhealthy and leads to a life of lax morals. A life that is in direct opposition to what God wants."

"I don't need a Bible lesson, Father. I want you to answer me."

"The deacons and I have been working with the local sheriff to bring an end to moonshine running in this county. We're shutting the Duval clan down for good."

"You can't legislate morality. I know you pretend to, but you can't. If people want to drink they'll just get liquor somewhere else."

"We can remove the temptation, and we will."

"I don't understand what your role is in this. If Boyd Cotton wanted to shut this down he doesn't need you." Lovey paced across the kitchen. This conversation was getting her nowhere.

"When these reprobates are brought to justice I will be on the podium with the sheriff, as a show of force. People will see that the church has power over their lives. They will be compelled to repent and seek God."

"Pride. That's what this is about. Pride and loss of control. You can't control people, and it makes you angry."

"I'll caution you to watch your tongue, young lady. And don't think I've forgotten that you said you were with Miss Duval last night. And according to Sheriff Cotton, that's not the first time. He'll see to it that Miss Duval is no longer an influence in your life."

Lovey knew that encounter with Boyd Cotton would come back to haunt her. She just didn't think it would be at Royal's expense. She'd been naïve.

"You don't get to control my life, Father, or who I spend it with."

"I've seen to it that a fine young man from the community has courted you and you will accept his proposal of marriage. I won't have a daughter of mine given over to an illicit lifestyle."

"Joe and I broke it off."

"What?" Her father's face contorted with the anger he was no doubt trying to keep in check.

"He knows I'm in love with someone else."

"I won't hear of this!" He slammed his hands against the table. "You'll tell him you made a mistake. You'll fix this right now."

"I will do no such thing." At some point during the conversation the power dynamic had shifted. Lovey found herself no longer on the defensive. No longer the timid child, seated on the church pew in awe of her father. It was as if she'd stumbled across the realization that she didn't need her father's approval. Especially if his approval required her to live a loveless life based on falsehood, just to keep up appearances. When his anger flared, she didn't flinch.

"Too often it may seem that the wicked prosper, but the flourishing of the sinful is an illusion. If you throw in with that Duval clan you will be lost and I cannot save you. In the end we are all the sum total of our actions. Character cannot be counterfeited."

"Indeed it cannot, Father."

"Thank heaven and earth that your mother isn't here to witness your behavior."

Lovey's blood boiled. To bring her dead mother into this simply to weight his argument with more guilt was the last straw. Her cheeks flamed with heat as she glared at her father across the kitchen table.

She went to her room, pulled a small bag from the closet, and began to shove some clothes and other small items into it. She stuffed the bag as well as she could on such short notice and headed toward the front door. She bolted past her father and out the door. He shouted from the porch as she reached the driveway.

"If you leave now. Don't come back! You will be shunned from this house and this family!"

She stared at him for a suspended moment, willing him to regret those words for the rest of his life. For surely she knew her own mind and her own heart, and she would return neither of them to this house. She struck out on the road back toward town to find Royal. A sense of urgency quickened her pace.

❖

Royal sat drinking coffee at her mother's table. She felt calm. For the first time in many days, she felt at ease with herself. She was stiff and a little sore from lack of sleep, but the night with Lovey had been magical. It had been as if they'd existed for a time in a magical cocoon protected from reality and sadness. Even though she would be mournful that they couldn't be together again, she was grateful that Lovey had come to her when she'd been at her lowest. When she'd needed her touch the most, Lovey had come for her. That had to mean something.

Maybe Lovey did care for her in her own way. Royal understood now that Lovey cared about her, but it just wasn't in her nature to go against convention. So Lovey would marry and have children, and Royal would go on with her life and look fondly back on their time together. The anger she'd been feeling had ebbed away with the soothing caress of Lovey's touch. It had been very hard to leave her sleeping in bed, but Royal didn't think her heart could stand to hear her say good-bye.

Royal knew she wouldn't be able to stay here either though. She knew if she stayed, watching Lovey build a life with Joe would kill her. Hers would be a slow and painful death. She'd been saving most of her cash. She'd make a break for it after tonight's run. Make a fresh start somewhere new, far from here.

"Where you been?" Her brother Teddy breezed into the kitchen, poured coffee, and swiped a biscuit from the skillet on the stove. He set the coffee down long enough to fold a piece of bacon over and press it into the biscuit.

"I've been right here all morning. Why?"

"No reason." He stuffed his mouth and chased it with a sip of coffee. "I got chores. I'll catch you later."

Royal watched Teddy lope out the door and across the front yard toward the barn. She'd sit and relax for another moment to finish her coffee then she'd head up to the still. She had no idea what sort of mood Wade would be in after laying his only son to rest, and she wasn't looking forward to finding out.

There would be no joy in making the midnight runs without Ned asking a million questions the next day about how the car performed. They had been a good team, she and Ned. She didn't know how she'd carry on without his friendship and support.

A knot started to rise in her throat. She took another swig of hot coffee to settle it. She didn't want to spend another day crying. She'd lost Ned and she'd lost Lovey. She needed to do this one last big run and start fresh somewhere far from here.

Lovey finally arrived at the dirt driveway of the Duval place. She'd already stopped at Royal's rented room and left a long note to say that she really needed to talk to her. She wrote that it was important and that she and Joe had broken up. She figured if Royal went back to her place and Lovey missed her, then at least Royal would know part of the truth. She'd left the bag full of her things in

Royal's room because she didn't think she could carry it all the way to the Duval place.

The house seemed silent, and no one came out to greet her. She covered her eyes with her hand to block the sun as she surveyed the area around the barn. The fog had burned off and the day had turned sunny, warm, and humid. The steam rising off the rain soaked grass almost gave the air the texture of a wet blanket.

Lovey felt she wasn't at her best. She'd rushed out of her father's house without changing or freshening up. She felt like a mess. And to heap insult on injury, she was frantic to talk with Royal. Just when she was about to lose hope, she heard a noise down at the barn and went to investigate.

The interior of the structure was so dark that it took her eyes a moment to adjust. She called into the interior, "Hello."

A scuffling noise greeted her hello, and a young man presented himself. He could have almost been Royal's twin, although his lanky youthfulness placed him to be a few years younger.

"Can I help you with something?" He pushed blond hair out of his eyes after he removed his sodden work gloves.

"Hi, I'm looking for Royal. Is she around?"

"She was. I just left her sittin' at the kitchen table a little while ago."

"Do you mind if I go and look for her?"

"Suit yourself."

Before she walked away, she turned back. "Are you Royal's brother?"

"Yeah, Teddy."

"I'm Lovey. Nice to meet you, Teddy."

"Likewise."

"I was very sorry to hear about your cousin."

Teddy lowered his head and nodded. "Yesterday was a sad day."

As Lovey walked to the house, she wondered why Royal never talked much about her brother. She'd mentioned him once, talked about how her mother babied him. Despite that, her first impression was that he seemed like a nice young man.

She stepped up on the porch and knocked lightly. No response. She pulled the screen door open and peeked inside. "Hello? Is anyone home?"

Lovey was beginning to feel like she was looking for a needle in a haystack. And the day was swiftly passing her by. It was probably past the lunch hour. She'd not eaten since the previous day and felt a wave of light-headedness.

She heard footsteps behind her just as she swayed a little on her feet. "Hey there, don't go passin' out on me!" Teddy stabilized her with a hand at her elbow. "Why don't you come in and sit down? I was just goin' to scrounge some lunch. Are you hungry? Do you need some water?"

Lovey nodded and followed Teddy into the house after he kicked off his muck covered boots.

"Take a seat and I'll fetch you some water." He primed the pump at the sink, sloshing water into a glass, and then handed it to her.

He took the leftover breakfast biscuits from under a towel and set a few on a plate along with some slices of cured ham, some butter, and blackberry preserves.

"Thank you. I think I do need to eat something." Lovey smiled weakly.

"Help yourself. There's cheese too. I'll get some from the icebox."

Teddy settled into the chair across from her. His resemblance to Royal was shocking and unsettled her a little. Where was Royal? She needed to see her badly.

"Do you know where I might find Royal?" asked Lovey.

Teddy studied her for a moment as if he was weighing how much to say to her. "You should eat something, and then I'll help you find her if she doesn't come back to the house. I've one more chore to see to down at the barn. If she's not back when I'm finished, we'll go look for her."

Lovey nodded. She was hungry and exhausted. They ate quietly together and then she settled herself into the porch swing to wait for Royal.

The shadows were getting long across the lawn, and Royal still hadn't returned. Lovey was emotionally spent, tired from her long walk, but anxious to talk to Royal. She decided to go find Teddy and pressure him to take her to see Royal. She didn't think she could stand to wait any longer.

She found Teddy behind the barn ushering a calf and its mother into a pen.

"She didn't come back yet?"

"Not yet. Listen, Teddy, I really need to speak with Royal. It's urgent. Do you have any idea where she might be?"

"I could take a few guesses, but she might be mad if I told you."

"It's really important that I find her, Teddy. I think she's in for some trouble tonight."

He seemed to consider her words as he closed the pen.

"I suppose I could take you there. We could go on horseback."

"I'm ready whenever you are."

CHAPTER THIRTY-THREE

Royal tested the foam cap on the boiler. Deciding the beer was ready, she secured the cap to start the process where the alcohol vapors traveled through the coil and then liquefied and dripped into the large pot. She knew it would take about three days for this next mixture to be ready for bottling. If all went as planned, she wouldn't be here to see this mix delivered. But she was going through the motions because she didn't want any trouble from Wade before she was ready to leave.

The sun was dropping behind the ridge when she began to gather things up. She had just thrown a bushel crate in the trunk of her car when she looked up and saw Teddy approaching on horseback. It only took a few more seconds for her to realize that Lovey was seated behind him on Midnight.

What the hell? She stood dumbstruck as Teddy assisted Lovey with her dismount. Lovey slid off the back of the horse, the hem of her dress catching against the saddle as she dropped. She quickly adjusted it after landing on her feet.

"Lovey, what are you doing here?" Royal couldn't decide if she was happy or angry. Teddy should have never brought her up to the still. Why had he done that? She gave him a questioning look as he turned his horse to head back down the hill.

"Don't look at me. She said it was urgent so I brung her to ya. She's been waitin' for you nearly all afternoon."

"Thank you, Teddy." Lovey brushed her hands against her skirt. She moved over to where Royal was standing, frozen like a statue.

"Lovey, what the hell are you doing up here? You can't be here. If my uncle Wade sees you he'll kill me and probably you as well."

"I needed to talk to you. It's important and it's urgent."

"Well, come on. We're not going to talk here. Get in the car." She ushered Lovey toward the car and pulled away quickly, heading back down the steep rutted roadway. After a few moments, she took a side road, and when she felt they'd put enough distance between themselves and the still, she pulled off the road and got out of the car. She began pacing back and forth in front of the car with her head in her hands.

"I can't believe this. Lovey, I can't see you right now. I'm barely keeping it together as it is. What are you doing here?"

"Defying convention."

"What?" Royal turned to look at her, mid pace. That she'd quoted the poem Royal had sent through the mail wasn't lost on her.

Lovey was beside her, matching her step for step until she stopped. "Royal, listen. You left this morning without me telling you that Joe and I broke it off."

"What?"

"Joe and I, we broke it off."

"Why?"

"Because I'm in love with someone else."

Royal stared at her. Hope surged in her chest. Could this really be true?

"Who are you in love with?" Royal had to ask because doubt wouldn't allow her to hope that the object of Lovey's affection might be her.

"I'm in love with you, Royal." Lovey placed her hands on Royal's arms. "I'm in love with you. I think I have been since that night I found you hanging upside down in your car."

"But…what about your father…what about all the things you said to me about why we couldn't be together? What's changed?"

"Everything has changed because I have changed."

Royal ran her fingers through her hair and blinked back tears. "Don't play games with me, Lovey. I can't take it right now."

"I'm not playing a game with you. I'm serious. I told my father that Joe and I aren't going to marry. He knows I spent last night with you." She dropped onto the wide front bumper of the car. "He told me if I left to come find you that I shouldn't come back. And so here I am." She looked at her folded hands in her lap.

Royal sat next to her, leaning against the front of the car. "I'm at a loss for what to say."

Lovey laughed. "I thought you daredevil poets had a line for everything."

"Apparently not." Royal leaned forward and put her face in her hands.

"Royal, look at me." Lovey stroked her back. "Look at me."

Royal turned toward her.

"Royal Duval, I'm madly, deeply in love with you. Please say you feel the same way about me. I'm so sorry it took me so long to—" Her words were cut short as Royal pulled her into a passionate kiss. They stood up, never breaking their kiss, with their bodies pressed fully against each other. Royal gathered the fabric at the back of her dress in her fingers and pulled her close.

"Oh, Lovey. I love you too." She whispered the words against Lovey's cheek.

"Listen, Royal. There's something else."

"Besides being madly in love with me?"

"When I got to the house this morning, Boyd Cotton was there with my father."

Royal pulled away so that she could see Lovey's face. "What?"

"They have some plan that I admit I don't fully understand, but the delivery tonight isn't real. They're trying to trap you and your uncle."

"Are you sure?"

"You have to believe me. You can't make this run tonight. That's why I had to find you, to warn you."

"Okay, listen, it'll be okay." Royal put her arm around Lovey and led her to the passenger side of the car. "Let's just get back to the house. I need a minute to absorb all of this and think it through."

Royal climbed into the driver's seat and sat for a moment studying Lovey. She wanted to believe everything that Lovey was telling her. Especially the part about being madly in love, but she worried that her optimism was too quick to accept this change of heart. As if reading the doubts on her face, Lovey spoke.

"I'm so sorry for everything I put you through."

Royal looked down at Lovey's hand on her thigh. She was worried this was all too easy. What about Reverend Edwards? Surely he wouldn't go down without a fight for his daughter.

"What about your father?"

"He'll either come around or he won't." Royal covered Lovey's hand with hers. "I only have one life to live, and I've discovered that I can't live it without you. I can't live my life for my father. I choose to live that life with you, if you'll still have me."

Royal pulled Lovey into a tender kiss.

They drove back to the house and were just climbing out of the car when Royal saw Wade appear at the door of the barn. They got out of the car as he approached.

"We've got a run tonight, Royal. A big one." He looked at Lovey but didn't say anything to her.

"My car isn't ready. The back is full of stuff from—"

"We're driving my truck because I'm not gonna risk this delivery in a car with only one working headlight." He scowled at Lovey. "And I told you never to bring her around here again."

"Wade, Lovey is staying here tonight. That's my decision and it's not open for discussion." Just as Wade was about to take a step toward Royal, her mother appeared on the porch, wiping her hands with a dishtowel.

"What's all this ruckus about?"

"Momma, Lovey is staying for dinner and maybe for the night."

Wade stormed past them toward his place. "I'll be back in few minutes to pick you up. Be ready."

"Why are we leaving so early? It's barely dusk."

"Just be ready when I get back."

They watched Wade's back as he disappeared around the corner of the house.

"Royal, fetch Teddy for dinner and I'll set another place at the table. You need to eat something before you leave for the night." Royal's mother was of the opinion that there was no crisis so large that it couldn't be resolved by the consumption of a good meal.

Alone in front of the house, Lovey urgently reached for Royal in the waning light.

"Royal, you can't do this run tonight. Not after what I just told you."

"I know."

"Are you going to say something to your uncle?"

"I should, not that he'll listen to me."

"He has to listen. They want to shut your operation down. I think they plan to put you in jail, or worse."

"Let me just think for a minute." She stroked Lovey's shoulders and arms trying to calm her down. She entwined their fingers as she spoke.

Before Royal had time to deliberate for long, Wade roared up next to where they were standing in an old truck. The wood-slatted truck bed was full and the contents covered with a canvas tarp. Wade stepped out of the truck but left the engine running. He had a sawed off shotgun in his hand.

"Royal, get in. You drive." He moved to the passenger side, never taking his eyes off Lovey.

"I'm not going tonight, Wade. And you shouldn't either." She couldn't stand her uncle, but she felt honor bound to at least try to warn him.

His gaze was like a vise grip closing around her throat. She stepped in front of Lovey, blocking Wade's view.

"I said get in the truck."

"Listen, Lovey came to tell us about an ambush. We should listen—"

"I ain't taking direction from the likes of her." He pointed in Lovey's direction.

"The likes of her is trying to save your sorry hide." Royal knew better than to raise her voice to Wade, but she couldn't help herself.

"I don't need savin'. Not by her and not by you."

"Wade, maybe you should heed Royal on this." Royal's mother had been standing on the porch watching the exchange.

"Woman, you stay outta this!" He glared back at Royal, jabbing his finger in the air in her direction. "Now get your ass in the truck or Teddy can take your seat. Your choice."

Royal bristled at the suggestion that Wade would take her younger brother along on a run that was surely not going to end well. Teddy was too green, he only ever tended the still, he never went on runs, and if trouble struck he'd likely be the first one to get hurt. She couldn't allow Teddy to go in her place.

Royal turned to face Lovey. "I have to go."

"No, Royal, please—"

"I can't let Wade take Teddy," whispered Royal. "I'll be careful, I promise."

"Royal, please," Lovey pleaded in a hushed voice.

"You stay here, Lovey. Have some dinner. I'll be back before sunrise. I promise." She kissed Lovey's forehead, then Royal climbed into the truck and Lovey stood, dumbfounded, as the vehicle spun around and headed out toward the main road.

She heard someone step down the porch behind her. She turned to see that it was Royal's mother. Lovey wiped at tears with the palm of her hand.

"I couldn't make her stay." Lovey watched the taillights of the truck fade in the dust.

"Lord knows I haven't been able to *make* that child do anything since she was five."

"I just can't believe it." Lovey began to pace as she hugged herself.

"Now there, everything is going to be okay. You just come in and have some supper. You're as skinny as a rail."

"How do you stand it?" Lovey still couldn't believe she'd failed to keep Royal safe.

"Honey, you can't control people. Even when you know what's

best for them." She wrapped her arm around Lovey's shoulder. "Come inside now and eat."

They entered the warmly lit kitchen and Lovey had the distinct feeling that she was lost in some bizarre dream. The entire scene was surreal to her. Royal was gone, and she was terrified about what was going to happen. And now she was just supposed to calmly sit and have an evening meal with Royal's family. Maybe this happened all the time in the Duval household. Royal would make a run and her family would act as if everything was going to be okay. Even though at any moment the car could miss a turn or be fired on by federal agents. How did they deal with the stress of it all?

"Well, who's this now?" A booming male voice pulled her from her mental musings.

"This is Lovey Porter, a friend of Royal's." Royal's mother made the introduction as she served each plate with yellow crookneck squash and fried okra.

"I'm Royal's grandfather, Duke."

"Nice to meet you." Lovey hesitantly took a seat at the table next to Teddy, who'd ambled in the door just now but had been quick to take his chair.

"Poppa, would you say grace?" Royal's mother settled herself into a seat at the other end of the table and reached out to clasp hands.

Lovey was comforted and at the same time unsettled by the warm welcome she'd received from the Duval family. Only a few hours ago, her father had been quick to dismiss the entire clan for low character, and in her opinion, he couldn't have been more misguided. They had shown her kindness and settled her at the table amongst them as if she were family, when in fact she'd been at the root of much heartache for the Duval household of late. Even still, they made no mention of it as second helpings were passed around the table along with a pan of cornbread.

"Lovey's father is Reverend Edwards." Royal's mother volunteered the information to Duke, who had been studying Lovey, but hadn't said much.

"You don't say." He entwined his fingers at the edge of the table as Royal's mother spooned more okra on his plate.

"And what's your skill, Miss Lovey?" Duke set upon his heaping plate again. "Besides turning Royal's world upside down."

Lovey nearly choked on the mouthful of lemonade she'd just taken. She swallowed with some difficulty and coughed into her napkin before she could speak. The old man clearly knew what was going on, despite his laid-back demeanor. "I'm trained as a teacher, Mr. Duval."

"Call me Duke. All my friends call me Duke." He smiled at her and refilled her glass.

CHAPTER THIRTY-FOUR

Royal downshifted into the next curve. The old truck had a high center of gravity, and she didn't like the way it swayed in the curves with such a heavy load. They hadn't been driving for very long when she began to argue with herself in her own head.

Why did she leave Lovey? Lovey seemed sincerely upset and she'd just gone off and left her to do what? Run a load of whiskey with an uncle she couldn't stand the sight of.

She felt guilt was the root of it. It was her fault Ned had gotten killed, and if she hadn't agreed to ride with him, he'd have bullied Teddy into it. He'd been a terrible father to Ned. And he would be just as cruel to Teddy.

And hadn't the woman she'd been pining over for weeks just professed that she loved her and her response was to leave? She must be losing her mind. Well, she'd done her share. She'd gotten Wade away from the house, away from Teddy. She was finished.

Royal slowed the truck and pulled off onto the grassy shoulder.

"What are you doin'?"

"I'm getting out."

"What?"

"You don't need me to make this run. I'll walk back and you can take the truck." Royal climbed out. She thought Wade would just slide over and take the wheel, but instead he walked around the front of the truck carrying the shotgun he'd had at his side since they left the house. Royal turned to look at him in the glare of the headlights.

"Get back in the truck, Royal." He raised the shotgun in her direction.

"What are you doing? Are you gonna shoot me?" She knew her uncle disliked her, but blood was thicker than water, and she'd never have thought one of her own clan would go so far as to turn on her to this extent.

"You're gonna get back in and drive this truck. We have a delivery to make."

"Why do you care if I'm in the truck or not? This way you keep as much of the cash as you want. Then you and Boyd can do your little backroom deals and leave me out of them." Royal started to walk away when she heard him cock the hammer on the gun, first one barrel, then the second. She stopped and slowly turned toward him.

"I'm sick of you and your queerie ways. I'm sick of the preference you enjoy because your daddy was the favored son. It's your fault Ned is dead." He took a step toward her, with the barrels raised. "You're gonna drive and that's the end of it. You owe me some respect after all you put me through."

Wade must have been out of his head with grief. That, coupled with his general ill disposition, was causing him to take it all out on Royal. Her mind raced along with her heart. The last thing she was going to do was climb back in that truck and face God knows what down the road with a man who clearly wasn't in his right mind. He'd have to shoot her first.

"I'm not gettin' in that truck with you. I'm done, Wade."

"You don't get to say when you're done. I say when you're done." Wade moved toward her with the shotgun raised. "Get your ass in and drive."

Wade took another step toward her, but just as he did, they both turned at the sound of a car rounding the curve in the road behind them. Headlights blinded Royal for an instant before she dove toward the shoulder on the opposite side of the road.

As the car slowed to move around Wade, who was standing near the center of the road, she used those moments to scramble up the bank under cover of thick mountain laurel. She heard Wade cursing behind her, and twigs snapped off along with leaf debris as he discharged the shotgun in her direction but missed her by about ten feet. Her heart pounding, she kept crawling up the hill keeping close to the ground until she found a dead tree to hide behind.

She heard him cursing and breathing hard as he tried to follow her ascent.

"Royal, you get back here. I mean it!"

She sank lower behind the tree, hoping he wouldn't climb any farther. Royal never got another glimpse of Wade, and after ten minutes or so she heard the truck engine come to life down below.

Holy shit. She leaned her head back against the old felled tree trunk and let out a long sigh. Lovey had probably saved her life.

Just to be sure, Royal walked back a little way, following the crest of the ridge. She wanted to see the truck actually head down the road and then she'd feel safe enough to strike out toward the house. The truck didn't drive off right away. Maybe Wade was waiting to see if she'd come back. He must really have believed she was crazier than he was. She kept walking just below the ridgeline until she could get a clear view of the road for the next quarter mile. What she saw along the road in the moonlight stopped her in her tracks.

At least four dark sedans were crisscrossing the road around the bend, ahead of where she'd pulled the truck off. Two of them she recognized as county vehicles. One of them was probably Boyd Cotton. The other two looked like the paneled cars she'd seen the federal boys drive. She hunkered down behind an old stump just as Wade's headlights crested the small rise and illuminated the blockade in front of him.

Royal's heart thundered in her chest at the thought that this trap had also almost caught her. She had a front row seat to what happened next.

Wade stopped the truck twenty or thirty feet before reaching the roadblock. He stepped out of the truck but stayed behind the open door. The engine was still running, and the headlights lit the gathering in front of him.

"We don't want no trouble, Wade," Boyd Cotton yelled from

behind one of the large forward sedans. "Throw out that shotgun and nobody will get hurt."

"Fuck you, Boyd!" The shotgun discharged and sparks flew across the hood of the car near where Boyd was standing.

Royal could see that Wade was ready to shoot again from behind the door. The shotgun was doing him no good at this distance. The barrels were too short; his alteration of the firearm for intimidation and short-range use were his undoing.

Boyd returned fire and Wade recoiled as the round caught him in the shoulder. He tried to raise the shotgun with his other hand, but before he could pull it off, two of Boyd's deputies were on him, wrestling him to the ground.

Royal couldn't believe what she'd just witnessed and how close she'd been to throwing her chance with Lovey away. She was shaken up and too afraid to walk along the road, so she skirted the ridge above the roadway all the way back to the house. It was late when she arrived.

She figured Lovey had probably gotten angry and left, and it would serve her right. She was berating herself as she approached the dark house when she heard Lovey call her name.

"Royal?" Lovey ran to her and jumped into her arms, kissing her all over her face. "Oh, Royal! You're safe!"

"Lovey, I'm so sorry I had to leave you. My uncle has lost his damn mind."

"Oh, Royal. If anything had happened to you I wouldn't have survived."

Royal realized her shirt was soiled and she had scratches on her arms from briars she'd encountered in the dark woods. "You waited for me?"

"Royal Duval, I would have waited on you forever. Did you forget the part where I said I was madly in love with you?"

Royal grinned. "I guess I was afraid I'd heard that part wrong."

They walked arm in arm toward the house, where it looked like only one light was still on.

"What are you wearing?" Royal looked sideways at Lovey.

"I took a bath after dinner and borrowed one of your shirts.

Your mother said you wouldn't mind." Lovey pulled at the front of the oversized shirt. She also had on a pair of Royal's trousers, which didn't fit her any better than the shirt. "I left some clothes at your other place. Maybe we can get them tomorrow."

"You're just making yourself at home, aren't you?" Royal put an arm around Lovey's shoulder and pulled her close, kissing her on the forehead.

"I hope I am home." Lovey leaned into Royal's shoulder as they walked toward the porch steps.

Royal stopped and turned toward Lovey, pulling her into a tender kiss.

They walked arm in arm into the house and up to Royal's room. She excused herself to wash up from her nighttime trek and then returned to find Lovey curled on her side, wearing Royal's shirt and nothing else.

Royal pulled the door closed and dropped her robe before climbing in next to Lovey.

"I feel like I'm in a dream," she said.

"Me too." Lovey caressed her face and then leaned closer and kissed her.

After they kissed for a moment, Lovey rolled on top of Royal, straddling her at the waist, the loose-fitting shirt falling open to reveal pale, perfect flesh underneath.

"Don't ever leave me again, okay?" Royal let her hands drift down Lovey's satin ribs under the shirt.

"I won't, baby." Lovey leaned over her and kissed her again. "I'm so sorry I hurt you. I want to spend the rest of my life making it up to you."

Royal pulled Lovey close so that she was lying full on top of her, bare skin touching bare skin. "I like the sound of that."

Chapter Thirty-five

The morning after Royal's late night hike through the woods, the Duval family received word from local authorities that after a short visit to the hospital in Gainesville, Wade had been taken into custody for the transport and sale of illegal liquor. Wade would be held at the county jail until his trial. His state-appointed attorney said, based on the sheer volume of physical evidence found at the scene and the fact that he'd fired on an officer of the law, that he expected Wade to be sentenced to some length of time, probably years, at the Georgia State Penitentiary.

Royal's grandfather had taken the news stoically and considered it a sign that it was time to retire from moonshining. Besides, Royal, his best driver, had announced she was leaving town to follow a different career path.

Two weeks had passed since Lovey had shown up on Royal's doorstep. It had felt like a dream, like a honeymoon. Well, as much of a honeymoon as anyone could have staying in the same house with your mother and a younger brother. Royal had moved her things out of the rented room right after Wade was arrested with the plan to pool all her cash for a place that she and Lovey would find together. And today was the day they were setting out to do just that.

They'd made an attempt to talk with Lovey's father, but he wouldn't even see them. Lovey left word with Cal as to where she'd be in Charlotte if her father ever decided to seek her out. She hoped he would, but she wasn't going to put her life on hold any longer just to please him.

Lovey carried out the last bag, and Royal added it to the things that were already in the trunk. She slammed the lid and turned toward her mother.

"Now you girls be careful and you write to me as soon as you're settled at your friend Dottie's, okay?" They'd made plans to stay with Lovey's friend from college, Dottie, and her husband, Richard, until they found a place of their own in Charlotte.

"We will, Momma." Royal's mother pulled her into a hug. Then Royal gave her brother an awkward, sisterly hug. Her grandfather was last. She clung to him for a few minutes longer than necessary.

He walked her to the driver's side of the car while Lovey said her good-byes.

"Royal, you're kin and I love you. I don't pretend to understand everything about your life, and maybe that's just as well." His voice broke a little with emotion. "I suppose I raised you to be more of a boy. And maybe that's because I missed your father so much."

"I think you raised me to be who I was meant to be."

"Now listen, I'd like to think I had a hand in who you turned out to be." He smiled and patted her shoulder. "Don't forget that I also raised you to think for yourself, stand up for those who can't stand up for themselves, and to take care of those you love." He looked in Lovey's direction when he said the last part.

For a minute, Royal thought he might actually start to cry, but he sniffed, wiped at his eyes roughly with the palm of his hand, and held the door open for Royal to climb in.

"I'm sure you've got better places to be than standing out here talking to an old man." He pushed the door closed after she climbed in, but the window was down. Royal leaned with her elbow through the opening.

"I've always got time for you."

Lovey climbed into the seat beside her. They waved back at those gathered on the porch as they pulled away from the house. It was early and sunlight bounced off the tall, dew-laden grass of the front lawn as they drove past.

"I'm sure Dottie can help me get placed in the school system in Charlotte. She said they're always in need of good teachers." Lovey placed her hand on Royal's thigh. "We'll be able to get our own place in no time."

They pulled onto the gravel road, and Royal shifted into high gear as the sedan gained speed.

"It just so happens there's a motor speedway near Charlotte where they do this thing that they call stock car races." Royal gave Lovey a sideways glance.

"You don't say. Funny you're just now mentioning this."

"I only just discovered it. And get this, they pay you to drive fast and you don't even have to carry moonshine."

Lovey laughed. "Well, I guess we both have a bright future waiting for us in Charlotte then, don't we?"

"I think you just might be right about that, Lovey Porter."

"That's another thing I've been meaning to talk to you about." Lovey shifted on the seat beside her so that she was partly facing Royal, her voice sounded serious. "If we're going to set up housekeeping together then I think you should start calling me Lovey Duval."

Royal grinned. "Yes, ma'am. I mean, yes, Miz Duval."

"Mrs. Duval," Lovey corrected her as she slid across the seat and leaned her head against Royal's shoulder.

"Who'd have thought? The daredevil poet and the bee charmer, riding off into the sunset together, living happily ever after."

Royal glanced sideways at Lovey. "Don't you mean sunrise? We are heading east, you know."

Lovey laughed. "Okay, into the sunrise then."

Royal put her arm around Lovey and pulled her close.

"I love you."

"And I love you." Lovey leaned over and kissed her on the cheek.

Royal turned the large dark sedan with the broken headlight and the dented fender northeast onto the main paved highway. The sun flamed brightly against the cloudless blue sky as it crested the ridge in front of them. It was the beginning of a glorious day, the first day of their new life, together.

About the Author

Missouri Vaun (MissouriVaun.com) spent most of her childhood in rural southern Mississippi, where she spent lazy summers conjuring characters and imagining the worlds they might inhabit. Missouri spent twelve years finding her voice as a working journalist in places as disparate as Chicago and Jackson, Mississippi. Her stories are heartfelt, earthy, and speak of loyalty and our responsibility to others. She and her wife currently live in northern California. Missouri can be reached via email at: Missouri.Vaun@gmail.com.

Books Available From Bold Strokes Books

Love on Tap by Karis Walsh. Beer and romance are brewing for Tace Lomond when archaeologist Berit Katsaros comes into her life. (978-1-62639-564-0)

Love on the Red Rocks by Lisa Moreau. An unexpected romance at a lesbian resort forces Malley to face her greatest fears when she must choose between playing it safe or taking a chance at true happiness. (978-1-62639-660-9)

Tracker and the Spy by D. Jackson Leigh. There are lessons for all when Captain Tanisha is assigned untried pyro Kyle and a lovesick dragon horse for a mission to track the leader of a dangerous cult. (978-1-62639-448-3)

Whirlwind Romance by Kris Bryant. Will chasing the girl break Tristan's heart or give her something she's never had before? (978-1-62639-581-7)

Whiskey Sunrise by Missouri Vaun. Culture and religion collide when Lovey Porter, daughter of a local Baptist minister, falls for the handsome thrill-seeking moonshine runner, Royal Duval. (978-1-62639-519-0)

Dyre: By Moon's Light by Rachel E. Bailey. A young werewolf, Des, guards the aging leader of all the Packs: the Dyre. Stable employment—nice work, if you can get it…at least until silver bullets start to fly. (978-1-62639-662-3)

Fragile Wings by Rebecca S. Buck. In Roaring Twenties London, can Evelyn Hopkins find love with Jos Singleton or will the scars of the Great War crush her dreams? (978-1-62639-546-6)

Live and Love Again by Jan Gayle. Jessica Whitney could be Sarah Jarret's second chance at love, but their differences and Sarah's grief continue to come between their budding relationship. (978-1-62639-517-6)

Starstruck by Lesley Davis. Actress Cassidy Hayes and writer Aiden Darrow find out the hard way not all life-threatening drama is confined to the TV screen or the pages of a manuscript. (978-1-62639-523-7)

Stealing Sunshine by Tina Michele. Under the Central Florida sun, two women struggle between fear and love as a dangerous plot of deception and revenge threatens to steal priceless art and lives. (978-1-62639-445-2)

The Fifth Gospel by Michelle Grubb. Hiding a Vatican secret is dangerous—sharing the secret suicidal—can Felicity survive a perilous book tour, and will her PR specialist, Anna, be there when it's all over? (978-1-62639-447-6)

Cold to the Touch by Cari Hunter. A drug addict's murder is the start of a dangerous investigation for Detective Sanne Jensen and Dr. Meg Fielding, as they try to stop a killer with no conscience. (978-1-62639-526-8)

Forsaken by Laydin Michaels. The hunt for a killer teaches one woman that she must overcome her fear in order to love, and another that success is meaningless without happiness. (978-1-62639-481-0)

Infiltration by Jackie D. When a CIA breach is imminent, a Marine instructor must stop the attack while protecting her heart from being disarmed by a recruit. (978-1-62639-521-3)

Midnight at the Orpheus by Alyssa Linn Palmer. Two women desperate to make their way in the world, a man hell-bent on revenge, and a cop risking his career: all in a day's work in Capone's Chicago. (978-1-62639-607-4)

Spirit of the Dance by Mardi Alexander. Major Sorla Reardon's return to her family farm to heal threatens Riley Johnson's safe life when small-town secrets are revealed, and love may not conquer all. (978-1-62639-583-1)

Pathfinder by Gun Brooke. Heading for their new homeworld, Exodus's chief engineer Adina Vantressa and nurse Briar Lindemay carry game-changing secrets that may well cause them to lose everything when disaster strikes. (978-1-62639-444-5)

Prescription for Love by Radclyffe. Dr. Flannery Rivers finds herself attracted to the new ER chief, city girl Abigail Remy, and the incendiary mix of city and country, fire and ice, tradition and change is combustible. (978-1-62639-570-1)